T0095586

THE PHANTOM
OF THE PALACE

THE PHANTOM
OF THE PALACE

BY JEFF MARTINEZ

BASED ON "THE PHANTOM OF THE OPERA"
BY GASTON LEAROUX

authorHOUSE®

AuthorHouse™
1663 Liberty Drive
Bloomington, IN 47403
www.authorhouse.com
Phone: 1-800-839-8640

© *2012 by Jeff Martinez. All rights reserved.*

No part of this book may be reproduced, stored in a retrieval system, or transmitted by any means without the written permission of the author.

Published by AuthorHouse   12/14/2012

ISBN: 978-1-4772-0635-5 (sc)
ISBN: 978-1-4772-0634-8 (e)

Any people depicted in stock imagery provided by Thinkstock are models, and such images are being used for illustrative purposes only.
Certain stock imagery © Thinkstock.

This book is printed on acid-free paper.

Because of the dynamic nature of the Internet, any web addresses or links contained in this book may have changed since publication and may no longer be valid. The views expressed in this work are solely those of the author and do not necessarily reflect the views of the publisher, and the publisher hereby disclaims any responsibility for them.

TABLE OF CONTENTS

Chapter 1
Hang Him High

FADE IN . . .

INT: VOODOO PALACE (STAGE)—NIGHT

The stage is dimly lit, but through the vague lights odd images mixing sort of gothic "Mardi Gras" masks with strange hoodoo symbols on the walls are seen. Skull candle holders outline the perimeter of the stage. Two tall, sloppily-set Tiki Polls stand high in the center each with two hooks to hang up a sign.

Suddenly, the house lights turn on, illuminating the joint as a tall lanky biker, JOEY BOUQUET carries a box of decorations, namely "Mardi Gras" masks and a banner. He plops them on the stage. He looks around to make sure that the poles and everything are set, but since they're not he straightens them out.

JOEY picks up the banner from the box, when all of a sudden the lights once again become dim. He drops the banner and looks around. A sinister laugh is heard faintly . . . as he looks around the laughter becomes louder, more threatening.

From a catwalk drops a black rope tied into a hangman's noose; the Punjab lasso. The maniacal laughter continues as JOEY stumbles around in grim awareness. His eyes squint in suspicion. He takes out a cigarette and just before his hand reaches eye level, the noose falls on to his neck and tightens as he's pulled higher and higher.

With his eyes bulging out like a bug's, and his fruitless attempt at loosening the rope, he kicks around in the air like a mule fighting with everything he has. He's finally pulled up to a cat walk as he stares in the blank, expressionless mask of the PHANTOM. A vicious smile comes across JOEY'S face as if he was not at all surprised by his death to be.

>   JOEY
>   I should've just kept quiet
>
>   PHANTOM
>   Maybe you'll you remember in Hell.

The PHANTOM grabs and throws his victim all the way down to the stage breaking every bone in his body and splattering his brains all over the stage.

The PHANTOM then takes a black rose from his sleeve and lets it float gently, silently near the dead body. The PHANTOM uses a remote to open up a trap door and JOEY falls in.

CUT TO . . .

INT: MAIN STAGE—AFTERNOON

A tough guy FBI AGENT JOHN MIFROID lights up a cigar and looks around the stage making sure everything's in order as the NEW ORLEANS POLICE is scurrying about. He sees some cops dragging the body in an opened body bag, and the bloody corpse. He cringes slightly.

He then walks up to the stage where a uniformed officer gives him an evidence bag with the flower. He holds it up to examine it.

> MIFROID
> This was near the victim?

> OFFICER
> Yes sir.

> MIFROID
> Any prints?

> OFFICER
> No.

MIFROID notices some other uniformed cop interrogating SIMON BOUQUET, the paranoid stoner brother of JOEY. After watching for a few moments, he walks up to the action and takes a seat by SIMON. He takes a long drag and stares coldly at SIMON. This is one no nonsense cop that SIMON'S dealing with.

> MIFROID
> What was your relation to Joey?

> SIMON
> I was his brother.

> MIFROID
> Did Joey ever do any feudin' with anybody?

SIMON
He got a little bowed up with us piddlin' during shifts, but wasn't nothing personal.

MIFROID
What about his past? Did he have any skeletons in his closet?

SIMON
Not that he told me. But then again, we were never really close.

MIFROID
Did he have any history of problems with depression?

SIMON
No. There was one thing. He kept talking about . . .

MIFROID
Something dangerous?

SIMON
This place is well, um, no. Forget that I ever said anything. You won't believe me.

MIFROID
I wanna know. Spit it out. I don't have all day.

SIMON
Well, it was some dead guy, man.

MIFROID just looks at him like he's crazy, while taking a long drag of his cigar.

SIMON
He looks like a zombie or something. Joey told me, himself. He has . . . his skin is extremely tight over his face, and he has a skin color that's a mix between puke green and piss yellow . . . It's weird.

MIFROID
Who do you think I am? Fox Mulder?

SIMON
I'm telling you, Man! It's that dead guy, Man! I know "drug" real from "real" real.

MIFROID
Uh . . . Yeah.

MIFROID just stares at Simon, pulls one of the other cops to the side out of SIMON'S hearing range.

MIFROID
It's just suicide. This redneck's just sniffing glue.

COP
Right away, Sir.

Chapter II
Superstition

INT: AVIAN KITCHEN—AFTERNOON

It's a bright place with this darkened Americana theme, a heavy pyschobilly influence if you will with a suitably dainty feminine touch added. This is any greaser girl's room.

A beautiful greaser girl seemingly straight out of high school, CHRISTINA AVIAN, sits at her table watching some poker tournament on TV. Like any modern day girl, her cell right next to her. Her phone gives a quick ring. Text. She picks it up and reads it . . . "Christina. Gabe. Claire's sick. Haul ass."

She gets the biggest smile across her cute little Americana face as she reads this news and replies back . . . "Awesome. On my way."

CUT TO . . .

INT: DRESSING ROOM—EVENING

GRACE SORELLI, a young gothic woman is minding her own business, carefully applying makeup.

When out of nowhere, a group of obnoxious little junior high rock-n-roll dancers just barge in like a stampede and slams the door shut like a victim in a slasher! Startled SORELLI jumps and the eyeliner slips and making a big line on her cheek.

> SORELLI
> Goddammit! Now, I have to start all
> over. I ain't never gonna work on

that stupid speech with all y'all
yapping in my face like idiots.

A red headed dancer (JAMIE) holds up her hands
as a white flag as she looks paranoid at
SORELLI.

> JAMIE
> Hold on there. No need to get all
> bowed up. It's just that we saw the
> ghost.

SORELLI stares straight in JAMIE'S eyes with
great cynicism as she lights up a clove.

> SORELLI
> Don't screw with me. Ain't no
> thing.

But all too soon, her cynicism turns into
anxiousness. She leans forward closer to JAMIE
and the other girls.

> SORELLI
> So you really saw that creep?

> JAMIE
> Ain't no different than me seeing
> you right now.

Then this black haired, Cajun dancer, MEG GIRY
shoves her way to the front just so she can
get her two-bits worth in the conversation.

> MEG
> If that was the Phantom, he's uglier
> than my Grandma's wrinkled old ass,
> Cher.

Once that's said, all the girls start
chattering about all these variants of the
ghost legend. SORELLI just stares in confusion
and annoyance.

One of the girls starts babbling about all
the places that she's seen him like she's the
coolest thing since video games. JAMIE just
rolls her eyes at the bragging.

> JAMIE
> Can it with all of the crap. You
> think every redneck you see is the
> ghost.

That dancer scratches her head with a little
birdie and cringes at JAMIE.

> DANCER
> Bitch! If you're so damn cool, YOU
> tell us about the Ghost!

As if paranoid about some government conspiracy,
she looks around a little TOO cautiously.

> JAMIE
> Well, keep it down.

INT: WRITER'S OFFICE—DAY

It's a crazy cool office with posters of all these rock operas, especially monster ones, such as STRANGE CASE and VAMPIRE A GO-GO. All these instruments crowd it up like Guitar Center. A weird looking, short guy with a taste for the macabre, GABE, sits at his desk writing some new rock opera. He has a cup of coffee on his desk.

SUDDENLY, there's a knock on the door. But still, GABE keeps pounding away on his keyboard.

> GABE
> Come on in.

ENTER THE PERSIAN, a tall, dark and handsome guy though totally mysterious. After a few more seconds, GABE stops typing and turns to the PERSIAN and giving this mysterious Palace patron a warm smile.

> GABE
> Oh, hey. To what do I owe the pleasure?

> PERSIAN
> Well, I need to ask you a few questions.

As the PERSIAN is speaking, GABE starts to get up but when he does, he knocks over his coffee and it spills all over the desk.

> GABE
> Damn. I'm sorry. Just give me a few moments. I will be right back.

Not wanting to keep a creepy guy like the PERSIAN, he runs out of his office's back door. And the PERSIAN just stares in grim realization. The PERSIAN lights up a cigarette as he awaits the return of GABE.

EXT: GABE'S OFFICE

The hoodoo Mardi Gras theme is even big outside the offices . . . Anyway, the PERSIAN waits outside leaning against the wall, just as JAMIE happens to be walking by. He gives a slight wave to her but she is really creeped out.

> PERSIAN
> Hello. You waiting for Gabe too?

She gives a nod, with fear that if she doesn't, he'll kill her . . . or something. Because of this he just shrugs in annoyed awkwardness.

> PERSIAN
> Okay, I'll shut up then.

From his office's back door, poor GABE staggers up with a bloody nose. Someone took a good swing at him. Out of great concern the PERSIAN and JAMIE run towards him. The PERSIAN sits him up at his desk. His face is a bloody mess. He's dizzy and out of it.

> GABE
> I saw . . . the ghost . . . and
> fell . . . as I ran . . .

    PERSIAN
    With a skull like face?

GABE nods and faints at his desk. The PERSIAN
turns to JAMIE.

    GABE
    Hey, can you get the house doctor?

    JAMIE
    Sure. Is Gabe gonna be okay?

    GABE
    Yeah. It's nothing. He just fainted.
    That's all.

EXIT JAMIE like a speeding bullet.

CUT TO . . .

INT: SORELLI'S DRESSING ROOM

    SORELLI
    Enough with the stories. I gotta
    redo makeup because of ya'll coming
    in here and creeping the hell out
    of me.

Just as she finishes up that long-winded
comment, there's a tapping at the door. They
all look at Sorelli, who gets up with a slight
sense of dread. She opens her drawer and gets
out a switchblade.

She doesn't really want to go answer it, but
what choice does she have with all those girls

starring at her? She conquers her fear though that is not what it feels like. She opens the door and slowly peeks out. She gets back inside, shuts the door and shakes her head.

>   SORELLI
>   There ain't nobody there.
>
>   JAMIE
>   That was pretty creepy.
>
>   MEG
>   It's the . . .

Just before MEG gets that last word out she catches her mouth.

>   MEG
>   Okay, I really have to shut up.
>   Forget I said anything, alright?

But none of the other girls, including SORELLI will have any of it. They are just too curious.

>   SORELLI
>   What the hell's that supposed to mean? Your friends ain't good enough to tell?
>
>   MEG
>   No, it means that if I sing I'm jinxed, okay?

JAMIE
Come on, Meg. You got us itchin' for
your tale. Don't be stingy with it
now.

Looking around as paranoid as JAMIE earlier,
she makes a crucifix with her finger. He leans
forward to tell her story.

MEG
Ma says La Fantôme don't like anybody
talking about him.

JAMIE (cynically)
Did your ma see Big Foot?

MEG
She's the one who keeps Box Five.
She always does this during a
performance. She always hears him.
Sometimes she chats with the ghost.
But she ain't seen him.

All of the girls including SORELLI look at
her like she's crazy, until Jamie's mother
is heard through the door. Jamie opens it as
her mother comes barging in like it's her own
dressing room.

JAMIE'S MOM
Did you all hear about Joey Bouquet
this morning as he was setting up?

The girls look at each other worried. Then
back at JAMIE'S MOM.

SORELLI
No. What happened?

JAMIE'S MOM
He was found dead. Rope around his
neck. Under the stage. The cops say
suicide, but they're idiots.

SORELLI
He was hanged?

JAMIE'S MOM
No. The cause of death was a fall.

MEG
Huh?

JAMIE
There are rumors of this garrote the
ghost uses to strangle his victims.
Tied like a noose.

MEG
Well, how would know anybody that,
Cher? How did the story get out?

SORELLI
Well, someone must have gotten out
to tell the story.

JAMIE
It started with Bouquet. Maybe a
failed attempt to kill him? What I
don't get was the fall.

JAMIE
Presumably, he tried hanging himself,
from the rafters, but slipped and
fell in the trap door.

JAMIE
That's a long shot.

MEG
Either way, I told you so.

CHAPTER III
REJECTION

INT: PALACE STAGE—NIGHT

The lights are dim and blue. Fog surrounds the ground. The seats are filled with an anxious crowd. Appearing on stage with a dark romanticism is CHRISTINA in a leather outfit. She grabs a microphone and the stage goes wild. Some heavy techno rock plays as she belts out JULIET'S theme from the Palace's variant of ROMEO & JULIET.

      CHRISTINA
      I would give you anything
      If you'd just stay with me
      I'll hold you through the night
      Oh baby, just say you're mine

      Please take this dance
      Come on, honey
      Let's make romance
      Oh baby, Oh baby [repeat 2 xs]

      I don't wanna ever let you go
      I just wanna let you know
      That you've the hypnotized me
      It'll break unless you stay with me

As she moves around, it's warm and romantic. It's as if she's truly in love with every guy that's there. Not just someone's who's only singing.

INT: PRIVATE BOX—NIGHT

A young, casual, nice looking guy with a subdued smile is sitting up starring at the pretty young singer. This is RAOUL DE CHAGNY.

His husky older brother, PHIL, brother is sitting by him while smoking a cigar enjoying the company and the playful flirts of a young lady snuggling up to him like a cat wanting to be petted.

RAOUL looks on in amazement at CHRISTINA'S performance. Almost shocked. He knows her. Without taking his eyes off of her, he elbows PHIL who looks up at him (though still caught up with the young lady).

    PHIL
    Yes?

    RAOUL
    Is that Christina, Christina?

    PHIL
    Where?

    RAOUL
    Onstage, dope.

PHIL takes a look on stage and sees CHRISTINA. He smiles as he remembers the times RAOUL and her spent together as children.

    PHIL
    Yup. That's her alright.

RAOUL
I'm gonna head straight down that
that there dressing room of hers.

PHIL (chuckling)
I thought I was the pervert.

RAOUL
You ain't got a lick of sense do
you, sex pot? I'm gonna invite her
to get some coffee.

INT: PALACE LOBBY—NIGHT

The place is crowded with goths and punks and
rockers here to enjoy the performances. It's
like a scene straight out of RETURN OF THE
LIVING DEAD. PHIL DE CHAGNY changed from the
young lady to the big time with SORELLI. RAOUL
is really getting bored, so he interrupts PHIL.
RAOUL shouts over to PHIL . . .

RAOUL
Earth to Phil! Anybody home?

PHIL sighs as he turns.

RAOUL
I'm going to Christina's room.

PHIL [a little surprised]
Do you know where it is?

RAOUL [blushing]
I kind of spied on her a few times.

          PHIL
          Alright. Have fun.

RAOUL runs off, and PHIL turns back to
SORELLI.

          PHIL
          Raoul and Christina had this puppy
          love thing going on when they were
          little tykes, and let me tell you
          something. It was so adorable.

SORELLI smiles at this comment.

CUT TO . . .

INT: CHRISTINA'S DRESSING ROOM—NIGHT

It's a nice place showing some of her Americana
though downplayed in respect for the owners.

CHRISTINA'S just wakes up as RAOUL comes in.
The few gothic and alternative dancers crowded
around her sigh with relief as does the doctor
that's there. RAOUL pulls the doctor aside.

          RAOUL
          Don't you think the place should be
          cleared out?

          DOC
          He's right. Scram so she can rest.
          (Turns to RAOUL) Don't worry, kid. You
          could stay with the new super-star.

RAOUL smiles at the doctor and turns to face CHRISTINA. The camera focuses on them while everybody else leaves the scene.

> RAOUL [kneeling down]
> Well, I'm the little brat who saved your black feather boa from the bayou.
>
> CHRISTINA
> Right and I am Bettie Page.
>
> RAOUL
> You have the same name and same features, and so it's pretty obvious it's you, but since you don't recognize me can I at least talk to you alone for a second or two?
>
> CHRISTINA
> When I'm better.
>
> DOC
> The new rock star's right. I have to give her a check up just to make sure everything's fine.
>
> CHRISTINA
> I'm fine. I'm just tired. That's all. I'll be fine in a little bit.
>
> DOC
> Okay.

RAOUL helps the DOC pack and they both walk out.

EXT: CHRISTINA'S DRESSING ROOM

The DOC and RAOUL close the doors and stare at the underground crowd. He lights up a cigarette while RAOUL just stands there thinking about CHRISTINA.

> DOC
> Stars; once they hit the big time, they treat the working class like crap [chuckles] and I'm only a nurse at the theatre. See you.

> RAOUL
> Uh, yeah. I guess so.

As the DOCTOR leaves RAOUL is about to open up the door to see what's going on but just as he's about to do so, his actions are interrupted by two voices, CHRISTINA'S and another MAN'S. Shocked by the voices, he decides to spy.

> MAN [o/s]
> Christina, you have to love me.

> CHRISTINA [o/s]
> How can you say that? You know that I don't sing for anyone but you.

> MAN [o/s]
> Are you tired?

> CHRISTINA [o/s]
> Tonight, I gave my soul and now I'm dead.

MAN [o/s]
Your soul is a beautiful thing child.
And I thank you. No emperor has ever
received so fair a gift. All the
angels in Heaven wept tonight.

RAOUL stands there and the bitterness in eyes
are in no way hidden. He hears a sound coming
from CHRISTINA'S room and moves just in time,
before CHRISTINA walks out of her dressing
room.

Once CHRISTINA is out of sight, RAOUL opens
the door to find that creep and to learn how
he got in. He storms in with a job to do.

INT: CHRISTINA'S DRESSING ROOM

It's pretty dark with only the light of the
hallway shining through. Through the darkness
even, it's a small enough room to be absolutely
sure there isn't anybody else in the room.
Still RAOUL is startled briefly, by nothing
more than a mannequin's head.

RAOUL
Are you hiding? I'm coming.

For a few seconds nobody answers, and Raoul
takes a seat.

RAOUL [with exhausted worry]
Oh god. I think I'm finally going
crazy.

RAOUL gets up and walks out.

EXT: CHRISTINA'S ROOM

He shuts the door and turns around to see
two guys in scrubs rolling a body bag filled
up on a stretcher to the lobby and talking
crap about their boss. Of course, RAOUL is
caught off guard, and starts to feel pretty
uncomfortable standing around some stiff.
Slowly, RAOUL approaches the two guys.

>   RAOUL
>   Um, what's that?

>   GUY 1
>   It's Joey Bouquet. They found him
>   underneath the stage a couple of
>   hours ago.

RAOUL stares at the body bag with some discomfort
since a stiff is right in front of him.

>   RAOUL
>   I'm sorry to hear that.

RAOUL'S eyes linger over the grim presence of
the body bag for a brief moment.

Chapter IV

Demands of the Dead

INT: PALACE SECONDARY STAGE—NIGHT

Even though it's secondary, it's still is a
fancy place with windows to the outside world.
It's one side of the Voodoo Palace's spectrum;
the mystical hoodoo aspect. Darker aspects of
Catholism mixed with bones, and weird cross
designs make the room eerie to anyone.

The alternative dancers are at their own row.
At the podium SORELLI is attempting to give
the speech for the evening's ceremony. She
seems ready . . .

>   SORELLI
>   Good evening, everyone. My name is
>   Grace Sorelli, and I am here to just
>   say how wonderful Jack Debienne and
>   Mike Poligny are . . .
>
>   JAMIE [o/s scream]
>   It's the Opera Ghost!

SORELLI sighs in annoyance and exhaustion.

>   SORELLI
>   Aw, shit.

As we see SORELLI get a little frustrated, we
turn to see a figure in a DAY OF THE DEAD mask
and black attire quickly run out of sight.
It's obvious that some stupid "clown" tries to
offer a drink to the figure, but the figure
was just too quick.

INT: AUDITORIUM SEATS

We catch two older guys, dressed in dark suits with gothic inspiration middle-aged perhaps, POLIGNY and DEBIENNE, checking their watches. They see how late it is and run to the stage to thank SORELLI who's annoyed by the fact that she won't be able to finish her speech.

EXIT POLIGNY and DEBIENNE

INT: PALACE DINING ROOM—NIGHT

It's the other side of the deal, total Mardi Gras. Masks and colors are all around. Portraits of king cakes fill the walls. The back of the stage has a Fleur-de-lis.

The dancers from previous scenes are dining with the older, slightly more provocative pinup dancers and the two former managers (POLIGNY and DEBIENNE) are sitting with the two new managers (MONCHARMIN and RICHARDS). DEBIENNE and POLIGNY couldn't really find anything out.

Suddenly, the figure from the last ceremony shows up at the managers' table. He decides to get himself a seat between the two sets of managers. It's as if a serial killer is taunting his hunter.

INT: DANCER'S TABLE

We see all of the girls but especially little JAMIE gets freaked out, almost but not quite in a speechless way. They chatter with silly nonsensical fear, like they woke up to find that they had their original noses.

INT: MANAGER'S TABLE

The managers stare at each other fear, in dread. They have no idea who this creep is.

>PHANTOM
>The cops are mistaken. I highly doubt that Joey Bouquet killed himself. I think that he was murdered.

>POLIGNY
>What do you mean?

The figure gets up, throw his right hand down, and smoke appears around the area he's standing in.

>PHANTOM
>He was found underneath the stage. Swinging by his neck as he fell.

The PHANTOM gives off an eerie laugh. When all the smoke fades away, the phantom is nowhere to be found.

>DEBIENNE
>Was he with you?

>MONCHARMIN
>Uh . . . no.

POLIGNY
Damn. Alright guys, let's go straight to the office. Like right now.

DEBIENNE
There's some final business that we really need to attend to before tomorrow.

RICHARDS [jokingly]
Like what? Some dead guy's out haunting this joint?

DEBIENNE
Well . . .

INT: MANAGER'S OFFICE—NIGHT

It's a pretty nice looking room, though much more basic than the rest of the Palace. Other than some posters and a few Palace trinkets on their desks, it's pretty plain. Still there is a big leather couch in the background.

RICHARDS and MONCHARMIN are sitting down, having a smoke. DEBIENNE and POLIGNY are pacing around worried.

POLIGNY
You guys need locks on every single door in this building.

DEBIENNE
Trust us. You will be very happy with those locks.

> POLIGNY
> If the Phantom has any request
> whatsoever, I suggest that you deal
> with it immediately in *his* favor.

RICHARDS starts to give a little chuckle while
MONCHARMIN smiles in vague amusement.

> RICHARDS
> We're smiling. Where's the candid
> camera?

POLIGNY pulls out a manuscript from the filing
cabinet with the fury of a madman.

> POLIGNY
> "The management of the 'Voodoo
> Palace' will give to the performance
> of the Rock 'n' Roll Hall of Fame
> the splendor that becomes the
> first rock opera in New Orleans,
> Louisiana . . ."

> DEBIENNE
> You ignore the rules you're toast.

POLIGNY hands to letter the two new managers.
Full of curiosity, RICHARDS picks it up. The
manuscript is printed in black ink, but the last
paragraph is printed in some faded red ink.

> POLIGNY
> There are four regular conditions.

RICHARDS
That's weird. "5. Or if the managers, in any month, delays more than a fortnight the payment of allowance of two hundred thousand dollars a month or two million, and four-hundred thousand dollars a year to the PHANTOM.

RICHARDS
Does he want anything else?

POLIGNY
Box five.

RICHARDS
The creep wants Box Five all to himself?

DEBIENNE and POLIGNY nod as if to warn the new managers not to screw around with this issue.

MONCHARMIN
You never thought about selling?

POLIGNY
Selling box five? Well, you guys could try it, but we don't know what the hell he'll do.

MONCHARMIN
Don't worry. We will.

With that, POLIGNY and DEBIENNE excuse themselves and go back to the dining room.

Once they leave, RICHARDS laughs hysterically while MONCHARMIN just stares at the wall.

> RICHARDS
> That was hilarious. Well, at least it's good they're leaving on good terms.

> MONCHARMIN
> They better not keep this shit up.

> RICHARDS
> Oh my god. Don't scare me, Aaron.

INT: MANAGERS' WAITING ROOM—DAY

It's the plainest part of the Palace. Just some cubicles that you would see in any movie about the workplace. An eccentric guy, REMY is typing away on the computer.

RICHARDS walks over to REMY to greet him. REMY gives him a box full of letters. The letter on the top of the pile has this weird black skull as an old fashioned seal.

> RICHARDS
> Remy who sent the letter with a skull?

> REMY
> I have no idea Frank. It was just there.

> RICHARDS
> Hey, do you know if Aaron is in the office yet?

REMY
Yeah, he's reading the mail right
now.

RICHARDS
Thanks, Remy.

RICHARDS opens the door to see a disappointed
MONCHARMIN reading through a nightmarishly big
pile of vague horror rock plots. MONCHARMIN is
bored stiff with the same stuff.

INT: MANAGERS' OFFICE DAY

RICHARDS dumps the box of letters on his
desk.

RICHARDS
Hey Aaron? Let's make this ghost
business into a rock opera itself?

MONCHARMIN
Andrew Lloyd Weber could do okay.

RICHARDS
Screw him. Alice Cooper.

MONCHARMIN [daydreaming]
Yeah, you're right.

RICHARDS
I'll let you get back to the mail.

With his mind elsewhere, RICHARDS gets the letter
sealed with the skull and he opens it. Once he
opens it, he rolls his eyes in annoyance.

> PHANTOM [Narration]
> Dear Management, I regret troubling you when you're so busy, renewing headlining contracts, signing fresh ones. Showing your great taste in general.

INT: MANAGERS' OFFICE

The poor managers keep signing away new contracts.

> PHANTOM [Narration]
> I'm aware of the generous deeds you are doing for Anna Carlotta, Grace Sorelli, and Little Jamie, not to mention some hidden talent.

INT: MAIN STAGE

A whore for the producers, she sluts around the stage looking for some action.

> PHANTOM [Narration]
> Of course, do not apply these words to Carlotta who obviously needs some singing lessons.

INT: SORELLI'S DRESSING ROOM

She's shaking hands with all these underground rock-n-roll greats.

> PHANTOM [Narration]
> Nor to Sorelli who's in the business due to acquaintances in high places.

INT: JAMIE'S BEDROOM—NIGHT

In her living room, she's watching some slutty pop music videos . . .

> PHANTOM [Narration]
> Nor to Jamie whose racy dancing unnecessary for a girl so young.

EXT: MANAGER'S OFFICE

She waits outside the office while the managers talk. When they come back out the shake their head in denial.

> PHANTOM [Narration]
> Nor to Christina Avian. Though she's the best, jealousy prevents her from her deserved fame.

INT: MANAGERS' OFFICE

The two new managers shake hands with each other pleased that business is doing well.

> PHANTOM [Narration]
> In the end, however, it's your business. Please run your business as you please.

INT: MAIN STAGE

Her performance during the former managers' Farewell party.

>   PHANTOM [Narration]
>   Either way, I'd like you to hear her
>   cover of *Romeo and Juliet*'s *Please
>   Take This Dance*. Once you hear it,
>   she'll become the reigning Palace
>   Queen.

The PHANTOM watches in the shadows as a young
couple steals his private box.

>   PHANTOM [Narration]
>   Please stop selling my box. It has
>   been repeatedly sold.

INSERT: FOUR MANAGERS

They discuss the mysterious Phantom.

>   PHANTOM [Narration]
>   I didn't protest since I assumed
>   the former managers had forgotten
>   mention my little requests.

BACK TO SCENE . . .

>   PHANTOM [Narration]
>   But I found that this wasn't the
>   case when I received an email I from
>   them. Still, believe me to be your
>   humble servant . . . The GHOST PS. I
>   attached a copy of their email.

>   RICHARDS
>   This is getting out of hand.

RICHARDS finds the printed email from the former managers.

> POLIGNY & BEBIENNE [narration]
> Dear OG;—There is no excuse for Richards and Moncharmin. We did inform them about you and we did leave your manuscript in their hands. Kindest regards.

> MONCHARMIN
> Let me take a wild guess. You just received the Phantom's letter. .

> RICHARDS
> Yeah, I did.

MONCHARMIN bursts out laughing

> RICHARDS
> These superstitious idiots are pissing me off. This prank has gone on for far too long now.

> MONCHARMIN
> Who the hell do they think they are? Just because they're former managers they think that we're just going bow down and kiss their asses?

> RICHARDS
> We're not idiots.

> MONCHARMIN
> Well, this seems harmless enough. The riddle is what their real motives

are, a box for tonight perhaps? For
whatever life they have left?

RICHARDS
I think it's a little deeper. They
seemed pretty interested in Avian.
She's supposed to be a superstar.

MONCHARMIN
I have a rep for knowing music, but
I can't tell c sharp from b flat.

RICHARDS
I say we give them the box and see
what happens.

MONCHARMIN
What's the worst that can happen?

Chapter V

Hating A Star To Death

INT: CHRISTINA' DRESSING ROOM—MORNING

CHRISTINA is applying some makeup carefully while talking to her "angel of music" the PHANTOM from behind the door. The PHANTOM seems like he feels a connection while, CRISTINA is bubbly like she's infatuated with this guy.

> PHANTOM [o/s]
> You did a splendid job, the other night. The crowd loved you. They went wild.

> CHRISTINA
> Not the entire crowd.

There is a pause and when the PHANTOM speaks.

> PHANTOM [o/s]
> What do you mean?

> CHRISTINA
> Well, I did read a review that said I was shit for Carlotta's role.

> PHANTOM [o/s]
> Who?

> CHRISTINA
> Some guy for the Hammer.

EXT: STREET CORNER—NIGHT

It's a dab, broken down street, the worst part of New Orleans' French Quarter district. Drab and dingy, graffiti decorates the buildings.

Bums and gypsies walk around begging for some spare change.

Out of the shadows, comes this figure dressed in black, using a leather trenchcoat to hide his face. It's the PHANTOM.

He spots a newsstand, with hardly a soul around it. Fast as a bat out of hell, he walks to the newsstand, slaps a couple of bucks on the counter takes late edition and runs off hurriedly.

He walks down a dark alleyway where the poorest of bums scrounge for food, like a bunch wretched scavengers. He gets a cigarette lighter and flicks it on, and starts reading the paper. The headline Reads "Christina Avian; A Screw up!"

> PHANTOM
> Though not total crap, she doesn't know about rock-n-roll . . .

With a fit a horrible rage, he takes the newspaper and lights it on fire and watches it burn. He storms out of that ally wanting that critic's blood.

EXT: NEW ORLEANS HAMMER—NIGHT

It's just this plain business building with nothing exciting about it, except perhaps, the edgy logo with a Thor like hammer. The place does, however, have all these vans presumably with equipment for a camera crew.

From out of the entrance this greaser with a dark edge walks out. He seems unapproachable and moody. Not the friendliest of guys.

He walks to his muscle car and drives off. As he does this, a weird looking hearse comes onto the screen as the eerie figure of the PHANTOM watches him . . . stalks him . . .

So this is the CRITIC who put down CHRISTINA'S beautiful work. The PHANTOM finds it pathetic.

EXT: ROAD—NIGHT

It's a crowded road. It's an extremely congested area. But at least it's the nice part of town. The hearse follows the muscle car, and it is sure keeping.

INT: APARTMENT—NIGHT

The CRITIC walks in and turns on the lights. It's a hell hole dump with beer bottles and ashtrays filled up all over the place. He seems more like he's a no talent hack. He has no right to talk crap about CHRISTINA. He locks the door. And turns on the TV. Some cheap old war film is on. That seems bad to. He leaves it on.

There's a loud knock on the door. Throwing a fit, the CRITIC stomps to the door and opens to see a strange figure with a strange plastic face, The PHANTOM.

PHANTOM
My name is Erik Ravenwood. I tried
to reach you earlier, but with what
your secretary said you are quite a
busy fellow.

CRITIC
What the hell do you want?

PHANTOM
Your review of Christina Avian has
troubled me. Perhaps I can treat to
a cup of coffee and discuss perhaps
seeing the show from a very private
box?

CRITIC
Hell no.

PHANTOM
In that private box. The acoustics
are better there. Just rewrite the
review. I'll make sure that you're
alone. You won't be disturbed in any
way.

CRITIC
I would rather die.

Now the PHANTOM'S really pissed off. He forces
himself in and pulls out a kodachi, a Japanese
short sword. He grabs the CRITIC by the hair
and shoves him against the wall and holds the
knife against his scalp.

      PHANTOM
      Your choice.

With near inhuman speed, he scalps the CRITIC as if he was slicing a piece of paper. He lets the CRITIC fall, and then he stabs the guy for some good measure. He throws a black rose on top of the corpse.

CHAPTER VI
THE DEMANDS AREN'T MET

INT: MANAGER'S OFFICE

MONCHARMIN walks in holding a letter from the Ghost. He sits down to open it.

>   PHANTOM [Narrative]
>   Dear Mr. Manager; Thanks. Charming evening. Day exquisite. Choruses want waking up. Carlotta, a splendid commonplace instrument.

>   INSERT: VAULT
>   —POLIGNY and DEBIENNE open it up and pull out a bunch of cash.

>   PHANTOM [Narration]
>   I'll write soon for my S2,400,000. Or $2,334,250 to be exact. The former managers already sent me my 65,750 for the first ten days. Kindest Regards, the Palace Ghost.

>   MONCHARMIN
>   This is getting out of hand.

REMY walks in with a telegram.

>   MONCHARMIN [annoyed]
>   What in the hell is it now?

>   REMY
>   I got a telegram. It's from the offices of the previous managers.

MONCHARMIN [sarcastic]
Great. Just what I need; another
headache.

DEBIENNE & POLIGNY [narration]
Gentlemen; Thanks you for thinking of
us, but we already informed you that
Box Five is off limits. It belongs
to him. Accept that and move on.

RICHARDS storms in slamming the door. He is
holding two letters.

RICHARDS [yelling]
Who the hell do those pricks think
they are; the gods of the goddamn
universe?

MONCHARMIN
Just shut up Aaron. Just shut the
hell up so we can think about this.
Clearly.

RICHARDS
What the hell do you purpose to do
about this pathetic little prank? How
much longer long will this last?

MONCHARMIN
Get Remy. He just might know a thing
or two. Maybe he's heard something.

EXIT RICHARDS and ENTER again with REMY.

REMY
You wanted to see me boss?

>   MONCHARMIN
>   Yeah. What can you tell me about the
>   Phantom.
>
>   REMY
>   It's said that he haunts box five.
>   Mrs. Giry is the attendant. Her
>   daughter Meg is dancer here at the
>   Palace.
>
>   RICHARDS
>   Get Mrs. Giry in here right away,
>   Remy. Tell her that we have some
>   matters to discuss with her. You got
>   that?
>
>   REMY
>   Consider it done.

EXIT REMY

RICHARDS lights up a cigarette relieved.

>   MONCHARMIN [with smirk]
>   Finally, we are getting somewhere.
>   I just hope that we could still see
>   the road after talking to this Mrs.
>   Giry.
>
>   RICHARDS
>   It's about time.

INT: MANAGERS' OFFICE

RICHARDS and MONCHARMIN are sitting back,
having a smoke and discussing plans for the show

during the MARDI GRAS show for this upcoming
year when REMY walks in with Mrs. Giry.

GIRY
I heard you wanted to talk to me.

MONCHARMIN
Yeah. What exactly do you know about
the ghost that just so happens to
"haunt" box five, Mrs. Giry?

GIRY
The phantom? Oh, what a great guy,
Mon Ami! The best customer I have
ever waited on.

MONCHARMIN
He's a nice guy?

GIRY
He gives ten to twenty dollars tip
if I give him good service.

RICHARDS
What services do you provide?

GIRY
I hand him his allowance along with
his program for the show. But I
don't get shit if some *idiots* sell
his box.

RICHARDS and MONCHARMIN look at each other as
if MRS. GIRY is a poor soul suffering from
hallucinations.

>   MONCHARMIN
>   Can you tell us what the Phantom
>   looks like?
>
>   GIRY
>   How should I know? He always wears
>   that Day of the Dead mask.
>
>   MONCHARMIN
>   Thank you, Mrs. Giry.
>
>   GIRY
>   Yeah right. Look. Just pay the guy
>   up.

EXIT MRS. GIRYMONCHARMIN and RICHARDS look at each other. MONCHARMIN takes a long drag of his cigarette.

>   MONCHARMIN
>   She must've been smoking way too
>   much dope way back in the sixties.

EXT: DE CHAGNY MANOR—DAY

It's a really classy joint, antebellum mansion. It's not real big or gaudy for a mansion though. Nice and simple. A bayou is seen on the side of it.

INT: RAOUL'S ROOM

It's a place of romanticized gloom. Think a room meant for Morrisey. All these poetic touches abound with sad love lost. Flowers and posters fill the room.

RAOUL is sitting at his desk, checking his email. His eyes bulge when he finds out that it's from his beloved CHRISTINA. He quickly opens the email.

> INSERT: COMPUTER
> —He received an email from his true love, CHRISTINA.

RAOUL opens the file and sees a heart with a banner through it. The banner says "Forgive Me." RAOUL pauses for a moment pondering if he should or not, but his curiosity is so strong as his heart is just too big. A tear falls from his eye.

> CHRISTINA [narration]
> Darling, I haven't forgotten you. I have to write today, since I'm going to Amosville tonight to visit my father's grave and Rosie. You know my dad really loved you. I miss you. Love, Christine

RAOUL turns. Seeing PHIL in the doorway makes him jump a bit.

> RAOUL
> Did Christina send you an email too?

> PHILIP
> Yeah, she did. Go get her, Tiger.

With those words as PHIL'S blessing, RAOUL rushes to his closet, gets out a suitcase, starts packing for his little weekend getaway.

CHAPTER VII
GRAVEYARD SEDUCTION

EXT: JACQUES' BAYOU BISTRO—NIGHT

A nice, quiet place right on the edge of a swamp, JACQUES' is the perfect place for fine Cajun dining. Murals of jazz and hip-hop leanings shine on the wall. But alas, it's pouring rain outside so Raoul is the only one out in the swamp trying to get to the restaurant. He finally reaches the mini harbor and goes inside.

INT: JACQUES'

The place is like club, but that doesn't matter. He walks in to see CHRISTINA at the bar drinking a shake. She smiles weekly at him as he hurriedly takes a seat next to her and smiles warmly right back at her.

    CHRISTINA
    Someone told me you'd come.

RAOUL gently takes her hands.

    RAOUL
    Who?

    CHRISTINA
    The spirit of my father, Raoul.

    RAOUL
    Did your father's spirit tell you
    that I love you something awful?

CHRISTINA gives a little giggle as if to be amused by RAOUL'S "daydreaming".

CHRISTINA
You're dreaming. I'm only 18.

RAOUL [a little irritated]
Come on Chris. I'm serious.

CHRISTINA
Raoul, I didn't come here to hear
quaint southernisms.

RAOUL [more irritated]
Oh, please Christina. You knew I'd
come running because of the email.

CHRISTINA
I thought I would remind you of the
games that we played as kids. Maybe
I shouldn't have sent it, but it's
just the visit to my room brought
memories.

RAOUL looks at CHRISTINA like she's crazy.

RAOUL
Be honest with me. Was my visit to
your dressing room the first time
you noticed me?

CHRISTINA looks down at the table with some
guilt.

CHRISTINA
No. When I was onstage and I did
see you a couple of times in your
brother's box.

RAOUL [almost yelling]
Then why the games when I reminded
you of the black boa, and why did
you laugh when I reminded you of
your boa?

RAOUL'S questions were so rough that CHRISTINA
just stares at him with so much hurt in her
eyes.

RAOUL
Alright, Christina. Enough is enough.
If you won't answer, I'll answer
for you. It's because there's some
creep who wants to screw you and
leave you. He's only looking for a
one-night stand.

CHRISTINA stares coldly into RAOUL'S eyes as
she lights up a cigarette, leans forward ready
to get right back at him for his jumping to
conclusions.

CHRISTINA
If there's anyone who's screwing up
our relationship, it's you Raoul.
Since all you're doing is barking
false accusations at me.

RAOUL
Yeah? What about that pervert creep
you were talking to after you told
me to leave your dressing room?

> CHRISTINA
> Who the hell's this other creep you
> keep bitching and moaning about?

> RAOUL
> The guy you gave your soul to.

> CHRISTINA
> You were listening behind the door?
> You asshole!

> RAOUL
> I spied on you because I love you,
> Christina.

Oddly enough, CHRISTINA becomes calmer with
those words.

> CHRISTINA
> So, what else did you hear?

> RAOUL
> He said that you had to love him.

Hearing those words, CHRISTINA becomes extremely
pale. Raoul becomes worried. CHRISTINA doesn't
look too good.

> CHRISTINA
> What else?

> RAOUL
> I heard your Angel of Music say,
> "Your soul is a beautiful thing,
> child, and I thank you. No emperor

has ever received so fine a gift. All
the angels in Heaven wept tonight."

CHRISTINA looks up at RAOUL like she's lost
her mind, and then her eyes form tears as she
gets clinically paranoid by the comment.

> CHRISTINA
> Listen, Raoul. I've never told a
> single soul what I'm telling you.

Curious, RAOUL looks at CHRISTINA. He leans
forward.

> RAOUL
> I won't sing. I promise.

> CHRISTINA
> Do you remember that one legend
> that my dad always told us, the one
> about the angel of music? It was his
> favorite one to tell.

> RAOUL [smiling]
> How could I forget? You always had
> your pa tell us. It was your favorite.
> In fact, I think the first time he
> told us was right here at Jacques'.

> CHRISTINA
> He also said here, "When I'm in
> Heaven, I'll send him to you." You're
> thinking I'm mad but I was visited
> by the angel of music.

RAOUL takes hold of CHRISTINA'S hands.

RAOUL
I really don't doubt that.

It is now CHRISTINA'S turn to look at RAOUL
like he's crazy.

CHRISTINA [puzzled]
And you actually get all this?

RAOUL
I understand that nobody could
belt out a song like you did at
the retirement ceremony, and that
no teacher here on Earth could ever
teach you those accents. You have
indeed heard the angel of music.

CHRISTINA [solemnly]
In my dressing room. That's where
the angel gives me my lessons.

RAOUL
In your dressing room?

CHRISTINA
Yeah, and I'm not the only that has
heard him either.

RAOUL
Who else heard him, Christina?

CHRISTINA
You did, Raoul.

RAOUL
I heard the angel of music?

CHRISTINA
Yeah. He was the guy that you overheard in my dressing room, when you were behind the door. I thought only one who could hear. Imagine my surprise when you told me that you heard him to.

RAOUL bursts out laughing. This action really pisses off CHRISTINA.

CHRISTINA
What the hell are you laughing at? You heard a horny pervert's voice, I suppose.

RAOUL stares at her trying to figure out how to word what he wants to say.

CHRISTINA
You were the one who said it. You were a friend of both me and pa, you're a rotten bastard. I'm not some whore locking herself up in her dressing room like some sex hotline. If you just opened the damn door, you'd have known!

RAOUL
But I did open the door There wasn't anybody in the room.

CHRISTINA
Well?

RAOUL
Well . . . I think that this angel
of music or whatever is playing mind
games with you.

CHRISTINA sheds a few tears as she gets up to
go.

CHRISTINA
I have to go.

CUT TO . . .

INT: FBI HQ [Interrogation Room]—NIGHT

It's totally dark, and then bright lights flash
on, where RAOUL is sitting asleep at a desk.
That and a couple chairs are the only furniture
in the room. A hand shakes his shoulder to
wake him up.

RAOUL
Where am I?

COP
Mr. De Chagny? I'm Special Agent
John Mifroid with FBI. You were
found knocked out at the Jean De
Saint cemetery on Hickory road. You
are currently at the New Orleans
Field Office.

RAOUL
How did you know I was there?

MIFROID
I was visiting my ma's grave over there, when I glanced over my shoulder and I saw you get the wind knocked out. May I ask you what you were doing over there Mr. De Chagny?

RAOUL
I was following a friend, Christina Avian. She's a singer at the Voodoo Palace.

MIFROID
Did Miss Avian hear your footsteps as you were following her?

RAOUL
No. She was way too wrapped up with whatever was on her mind.

MIFROID
I see. Could you please tell me what you remember?

EXT: JEAN DE SAINT CEMETERY—DAY

Fog fills the cemetery. Hardly anything is visible. It's your classic gothic cemetery other than the fact that the graves are above ground heightening the creepy factor. This is Louisiana.

CHRISTINA looks around making sure that had nobody followed her. Once she's sure, she walks closer and closer to the elegant mausoleum. Staying out her view, RAOUL follows her. From the mausoleum, some faint romantic male singing with some guitar accompaniment plays.

> MIFROID [interrupting (v/o)]
> Were you able to see this guy's face?

> RAOUL [v/o]
> No.

> MIFROID [v/o]
> Alright, go on.

Near this tree, are piles of presumably dug up heads. RAOUL looks freaked out by this but it doesn't stop him. As he moves closer and closer, it seems more and more like CHRISTINA'S in a trance.

Suddenly, out of nowhere, some guy starts throwing skulls near RAOUL. At first he pays no mind . . .

That is until someone actually hits his head. He turns around and sees this creep in dark suit with some kind of skull mask. The creep gives RAOUL a cold hard punch.

BACK TO INTERROGATION ROOM . . .

> MIFROID
> Alright, Mr. De Chagny. You can go now. I'll have one of my guys drop you off at the cemetery so you could get back to your car.

RAOUL
What? Just like that. I could just
walk myself out of here?

MIFROID
We weren't holding you, Mr. de
Chagny.

RAOUL
Then what the hell am I doing here?

MIFROID
I was just being a good Samaritan,
Mr. de Chagny.

RAOUL
Alright.

EXIT RAOUL

Chapter VIII

Carlotta's Fall

INT: MANAGERS' OFFICE—AFTERNOON

MONCHARMIN and RICHARDS are pacing back and fourth kind of anxious or something.

>   RICHARDS
>   Maybe those potheads are right.

>   MONCHARMIN
>   Don't tell me you buy it.

>   RICHARDS
>   I have a feeling that there's some psycho who wants to run this joint and turn into it into his own private hell-house.

>   MONCHARMIN
>   As crazy as that may sound, it actually does sound like a reasonable explanation.

>   RICHARDS
>   Think about it. Ever since Joey Bucket has found hanging, with all of the rumors from the staff, I have hard time buying two former managers could put together a practical joke this elaborate.

Suddenly, REMY bursts through the door.

>   RICHARDS
>   Can we help you?

                REMY
                Someone just stole a Specter.

                RICHARDS
                What are you saying?

                REMY
                I mean that some freak dressed like
                some dead biker from beyond the
                grave just ripped off one of our
                white specter Harley Davidsons.

                RICHARDS
                Alright, then. Call FBI Field
                Office and ask for Special Agent
                John Mifroid. He was the guy who
                they sent check out the Joey Bouquet
                suicide just the other day.

                REMY
                Sure thing, boss.

REMY walks out the door while a girl wearing a
nice skirt and blazer walks over to MONCHARMIN
and RICHARDS with a deep annoyance.

                LADY
                What is this pathetic thing that
                Christina Avian wrote to Anna
                Carlotta?

                MONCHARMIN
                First of all, Lady, who the hell are
                you? And second, what the hell are
                you babbling about?

LADY
I'm Nina, Anna Carlotta's PA and I'm
talking about this letter.

SATO hands the letter to Moncharmin who rips
it open.

PHANTOM [Narration]
Carlotta, You'll claim to be ill
during Faust; in order to have
Christina Avian take your place.
If you decline from doing so, be
prepared for a great misfortune once
you open your mouth.

MONCHARMIN turns to RICHARDS.

MONCHARMIN
A nutcase wants to run our show.

RICHARDS
Allow Carlotta to sing her part.
Nothing will happen to her.

NINA
Alright, but nothing, *nothing* can
happen to her. Do you understand me?

MONCHARMIN
Yes, Miss Sato. Loud and clear.

EXIT NINA

RICHARDS
Well, physically, I think Carlotta
will be fine. It's the "worse than

death" part that's getting me a
little worried.

MONCHARMIN
It could mean that Anna Carlotta
will somehow make a complete and
utterly humiliating mistake onstage.
I have a hard time believing that
the Madonna of rock operas could
handle making a mistake.

RICHARDS [mock dread]
Oh, no! I made a mistake! I'm
doomed.

The two managers burst out in laughter.

RICHARDS
Oh, god. We would be the laughing
stock of the New Orleans rock opera
scene. And that is not something I
wanna go through.

CUT TO . . .

INT: PHIL'S HOME OFFICE—AFTERNOON

It's a cozy place, very calm and serene.
There are a lot of inspirational posters and
paintings, yet it seems perfectly suitable for
a business office.

PHIL is sitting at his desk, checking some
email. He notices an email from CHRISTINA. The
subject title is "Thank You". PHIL decides to
open it.

CHRISTINA [narration]
Phil, How are you and Raoul? Anyway,
I'm aware of you putting in a good word
for me. Thank you. I really appreciate
it. But, I'd rather work up to the
top on my own. Thanks anyway.

PHIL [to himself]
But I haven't been talking to the
managers. Huh. That's weird.

CUT TO . . .

INT: CARLOTTA'S DRESSING ROOM—EVENING

The dressing room has a darker, more liberal
tone than CHRISTINA'S. It looks like some
zombie whore's room, with slutty horror pinup
posters. To top it all off, the place is a
mess. Clothes and underwear are thrown about
like rag dolls in riot.

CARLOTTA'S is preparing for the night's
performance. SATO is watching her with great
approval.

CARLOTTA
Are you sure that nothing will happen
to me while I'm up there, Nina?

NINA
Positive.

CARLOTTA
Good. I don't want some psycho making
me look like a freak.

CUT TO . . .

INT: BACKSTAGE—EVENING

People scurry about, both cast and crew. It's a colorful place, but very chaotic. Nobody is lying about like a lazy bum.

There is some table with a whole bunch of bottles of drinks. One is marked "ANNA CARLOTTA". A gloved hand moves closer to the bottle.

The dark figure of the PHANTOM pours a clear liquid into the bottle. He then broods away from the scene of the crime laughing moodily.

INT: BOX FIVE—NIGHT

RICHARDS and MONCHARMIN are sitting there a little anxious. They know that something's up. They look at each other with grim worry.

    RICHARDS
    Nothing better happen tonight.

    MONCHARMIN
    Nothing will happen to Carlotta. The
    note said a fate worse than death.
    What's that going to be, Frank, a little
    splat of ketchup on her costume?

    RICHARDS
    Something's up. I can feel it.

    MONCHARMIN
    Come on. Let's go get drunk.

With that, the two exit Box Five.

INT: CARLOTTA'S DRESSING ROOM NIGHT

CARLOTTA is sitting and putting on way too much prostitute like makeup. She's already in costume, and it covers only a little. Her little aid gives her a note with the PHANTOM'S skull sealing it in the envelope. Of course, CARLOTTA doesn't appreciate it.

    CARLOTTA
    What in the hell is that, Maria?

    MARIA
    I don't know. I just found it on the
    ground.

    CARLOTTA
    "Found it on the ground." That's
    bullshit and you know it. Just give
    it to me.

She reads the Phantom's letter.

    GHOST [narrative]
    If you are smart, you will see that
    it is insanity to try and perform
    tonight.

BACK TO SCENE . . .

    CARLOTTA [screaming]
    NINA! Get your fat ass over here
    now!

NINA lazily walks over to CARLOTTA.

> NINA
> Yes, Anna?
>
> CARLOTTA
> Burn this piece of crap.

NINA receives the note from CARLOTTA and sets it over a candle. She gives MARIA a "here we go again" look.

INT: BOX FIVE—NIGHT

RICHARDS and MONCHARMIN return to the box with some wine, and they notice a small metal package.

> MONCHARMIN
> What is that metal thing there?
>
> RICHARDS
> A box of chocolates. Call Mrs. Giry.

MONCHARMIN walks up to the entrance of the box. He and MRS. GIRY walk in as RICHARDS opens the package to find a variety of chocolate candies.

> GIRY
> Oui?
>
> RICHARDS
> Where did this package of chocolates come from, Mrs. Giry? Tell us now.

GIRY
Don't ask me. I'm just the guard to
this box.

RICHARDS
Don't play games with me, damn it!
Tell me where they came from!

GIRY
How am I supposed to know? My only
guess is the phantom.

MONCHARMIN
We can figure this out after.

RICHARDS begrudgingly puts back all of his
attention to the night's performance.

INT: PALACE MAIN STAGE—NIGHT

The house lights turn slowly off as the lights
on stage turn on just as slowly. We see a
performance of EDDIE NELSON as JOHNNY FAUST.

STAGE NARRATOR
Hello, everyone. This is the tale of
Johnny Faust. He was a lonely man in
a lonely town who sold is soul to
the devil.

LATER ONSTAGE

Some new wave plays as CHRISTINA comes to sing
her part.

> CHRISTINA [Song]
> *I remember you from so long ago*
> *Playing at the bebop a go-go*
> *So, come back with me, baby?*
> *To the rock-n-roll. Be my king?*
> *All I want is to love you . . .*

With that last line, her performance gets real flat.

> CHRISTINA [Song]
> *So, why don't you please love 'til the end of time? I'll be yours and you'll be mine.*

She repeats the chorus a couple of times, but as she does this the audience sees how uninterested she is in her part.

LATER ONSTAGE

The stage changes into a more hellish setting. EDDIE'S character looks around in horror as some '70s doom metal blasts play slowly and threateningly from the orchestra type rock band. CARLOTTA'S character [second only to the devil himself] rises from a great ball of fire that shoots out from a trap door below the stage. She walks over to EDDIE'S character like she wants to get some action from him.

> CARLOTTA [singing]
> *Johnny. What can I get you honey? I can grant you about anything Your little heart desires.*

"Your little heart desires" Sounds like it's croaked from a frog. Everybody in the audience is shocked.

>   CARLOTTA [singing]
>   *If you'll burn in my fire . . .*

". . . Burn in my fire" is croaked as well, and CARLOTTA gets a horrid stomach ache as she pukes all over the stage. The sight of the puke causes her to faint and fall into the trap door.

CUT TO . . .

INT: BOX FIVE—NIGHT

MONCHARMIN is stunned while RICHARDS just looks gloomily into space.

>   RICHARDS
>   So, this is what the Opera ghost meant.

A hideous laugh is heard throughout the entire opera. It's the Palace ghost.

>   PHANTOM [o/s echoing]
>   She's singing to bring down the chandelier . . .

The PHANTOM just laughs for the entire rest of the scene. A dark, creepy looking chandelier out of a Tim Burton movie.

You see the audience around a beautifully macabre chandelier. The camera moves up to the top of the rope that's holding the chandelier together. You see that the chord is dangerously loose.

    PHANTOM[o/s]
    She's singing to bring down the chandelier!

You see the chandelier fall, the audience screams and they run, all except CARLOTTA'S good friend JACKIE STEVENS. JACKIE is just paralyzed with fear. She can't even scream.

INT: CAVE—NIGHT

The fainted body of CARLOTTA lies with puke and bruises all over her. The only light is from a lantern on the ground.

The menacing PHANTOM walks slowly up to her with a switchblade knife. He slaps CARLOTTA awake. She screams at the blank expressionless boogeyman. He backhands her so she would shut up, which she does.

    PHANTOM
    So, how's everybody's favorite bitch whore?

    CARLOTTA
    Go to Hell, you filthy old bastard.

    PHANTOM
    Sorry, Babe. Been there, done that.

The PHANTOM pulls out some handcuffs, and waves them around as if to mock CARLOTTA'S whorish persona.

                    CARLOTTA
          What the hell are those things for?

                    PHANTOM
          Uh . . . bondage?

                    CARLOTTA
          I charge 20 bucks an hour.

                    PHANTOM
          Ooh. Not expensive. Well, it's not
          that kind of deal, honey.

The PHANTOM cuffs her, and starts waving his switchblade as if he were playing some kinky game. Dancing around he giggles seductively at her. He ends up slashing her lower neck a couple of time, nonchalantly as if it's just something to do. He uses her hair to wipe off the blood on the knife.

                    CARLOTTA
          You lousy bastard! That really hurt!
          I could sue your cheap psycho ass.

                    PHANTOM
          Here's the deal. Go down to Baton
          Rouge. Live the happy life of the
          slut you are. Let Christina Avian
          have the spotlight here.

CARLOTTA
If I refuse?

PHANTOM
You'll just have to find out, won't
you?

CARLOTTA
Then Hell no!

In a flying fit of rage, he takes his switchblade
and repeatedly, maniacally shoves it right
into her heart until she's nothing more than a
mutilated corpse. Checking all directions he
flees the scene.

Chapter IX

More Confusion

INT: MANAGER'S OFFICE—LATE NIGHT

RICHARDS and MONCHARMIN pace around frantically.

> MONCHARMIN
> What the hell are we going to do, Frank?

> RICHARDS
> Remember what the Phantom said about the chandelier?

RICHARDS walks over to his desk. There is a bundle of paperwork on there. He picks up a certain manila folder. He opens it and scams through it.

> INSERT: FOLDER CONTENTS
> —There are some pretty graphic pictures of the body of Jackie Stevens.

BACK TO SCENE

He puts the folder back with great rage.

> RICHARDS [firmly]
> That psycho is playing with madness and we will not let him do that. Do you understand me?

CUT TO . . .

MONCHARMIN nods.

INT: DE CHAGNY DINING ROOM—MORNING

RAOUL walks into the dining room only to see a very upset PHIL, who looks up at RAOUL and throws a note at him.

>RAOUL
>What is this?

>PHIL
>Look.

>RAOUL
>Who's it from?

>PHIL
>It's from that filthy singing whore.

RAOUL can only look at PHIL in confusion.

>RAOUL
>What's going on?

>PHIL
>I'm talking about Christina Avian, Raoul.

>RAOUL
>What about Christina?

>PHIL
>Read the letter. You'll find out.

RAOUL opens up the letter.

>   CHRISTINA [narrating]
>   Baby, I'm so sorry, but you have to
>   forget about me. Our lives depend on
>   it. Your Little Lottie

RAOUL drop his head into his hands with great sadness. Tears begin to fall from his broken-hearted face. He turns to PHIL who looks just as sad.

>   PHILIP
>   I am so sorry, Raoul.

>   RAOUL
>   I have to go see Valerie, Philip.

>   PHILIP
>   Isn't that the sweet old lady who
>   adopted Christina?

>   RAOUL
>   Yeah. There's something really weird
>   going on.

RAOUL lights up a cigarette.

EXT: SWAMP SIDE HOUSE—AFTERNOON

It's a classic voodoo house with catholic imagery all around, and some basic Cajun styles.

RAOUL walks up to the door, and rings the doorbell. A couple of minutes later, the door is answered by a Cajun Gypsy lady. This is

VALERIE. She smiles at RAOUL who smiles back.
It's obvious that they know each other.

> VALERIE
> Raoul, to what do I owe the
> pleasure?

> RAOUL
> Valerie, I am sorry it couldn't be
> under more joyful circumstances, but
> the reason why I'm here is to talk
> to you about Christina.

> VALERIE
> Christina. Well, come in, Raoul.

RAOUL does as much.

INT: VALERIE'S LIVING ROOM

It's a nice place. It's not big, but it has
a pleasant, calm atmosphere. There's a lot
of love in the room. RAOUL and VALERIE are
drinking some coffee.

> RAOUL
> I need to know where Christina is.

> VALERIE
> Why, she is with her singing
> instructor, the angel of music. Now,
> make sure that you don't repeat what
> I'm about to you to anyone. Or it'll
> all be for nothing, ya hear?

RAOUL
You can count on me, Val.

VALERIE gives him a warm motherly smile.

VALERIE
You're perfect for her.

RAOUL
What makes you think that?

VALERIE
Well, she used to tell me about how warm and thoughtful you were, not to mention how "hot". But did you actually think that she was free?

RAOUL
"Free"? What the hell does that mean? Is Christina engaged?

VALERIE
No, of course not, Child. The angel of music wouldn't let her.

RAOUL [skeptical]
The angel of music won't let her get married?

VALERIE
She told me that if the angel of music would ever catch her getting married, that he is forever out of the picture. But I thought Christina told you not to long ago, the night at the cemetery.

RAOUL
Valerie, tell me where he lives.

VALERIE
In Heaven.

RAOUL
Well how long has Christina been acquainted with him?

VALERIE
He started three months ago.

RAOUL
Where does he give her the lessons?

VALERIE
He used to give her the lessons in her dressing room, but ever since she first gone with him, I don't know.

CUT TO . . .

EXT: RECORD STORE—NIGHT

It's a very eclectic store. All these punk rock and new wave artists are painted on the wall.

RAOUL is walking out, when he sees a black hearse drive by. He could have sworn that CHRISTINA was in the back passenger's seat, but whoever was sitting there with who looked like CHRISTINA, rolled up the window before RAOUL could be certain.

CUT TO . . .

INT: RAOUL'S BEDROOM—NIGHT

RAOUL goes up to his computer to check if he
has any important email. He finds that he has
received an email from his beloved CHRISTINA.

>   CHRISTINA [Narrative]
>   Honey, Go to the Mardi Gras Party
>   the night after tomorrow. Wear your
>   Jester costume. Meet me in the small
>   room behind the meeting room. Do not
>   say anything to anyone about this.
>   Love Christina
>
>   RAOUL [to himself]
>   Christina, what did you get yourself
>   into? How did some guy drag you away?
>   Please don't play a cruel game with
>   me.

CHAPTER X

DEATH WEARS RED

Jeff Martinez

INT: PALACE LOBBY—NIGHT

All these clowns and masks abound the halls and walls. Color and the festive attitude is playfully contagious.

The Mardi Gras party has a wide arrange of wild costumes. Everybody is dancing around, enjoying drinks and food. RAOUL is there in the classic court jester costume that CHRISTINA told him to be in. He keeps pacing around checking his watch. Some festive music plays.

> RAOUL
> Damn. It's only eleven fifteen. And I still have forty-five minutes to go.

As he says this, a figure in a creepy red suit broods around. He has a skull-shaped mask on. It has a rotting, skull with a horrid "juicy" design as if the skull is still fresh. In the back of his red trenchcoat are the words "RED DEATH—TOUGH ME AND DIE!" A big chubby guy trying to be a badass walks up to him and taps his shoulder. RED DEATH grabs the hand with great fury squeezing all the air out of the poor guy.

> RED DEATH
> I suggest you don't do that again, or you won't like me very much, do I make myself clear you oversized beach ball?

RED DEATH lets go and walks away. The big guy holds his arm. He looks really creeped out. RAOUL'S watch says 12:00 am. He rubs his forehead in relief.

>RAOUL
>Well, it's time.

EXIT RAOUL . . .

INT: PALACE LOBBY STAIRCASE

RAOUL climbs up the steps one by one. He's not taking his time, but he's not quite in a rush, either. A servant offers RAOUL something to drink, but RAOUL refuses.

INT: MEETING ROOM

The camera follows Raoul all around the room. It's like a psychedelic lizard lounge. There are all these cheetah print couches and martini murals. RAOUL makes it to the other door, and he enters the small multi-purpose room.

INT: MULTIPURPOSE ROOM

It looks more gothic in this room than it does psychedelic like it did in the other room. RAOUL finds a girl in a creepy black dress with a long black veil over her face standing at the far end of the room. RAOUL walks up to the dark figure.

>   RAOUL
>   Christina is that . . .

The girl puts her index finger on his lips to shush him up. Then she signals him to follow her. A figure in red is seen for a split-second by RAOUL.

INT: OPERA BOX

RAOUL and CHRISTINA enter. CHRISTINA is very cautious. RAOUL senses that there's something up with that girl.

>   CHRISTINA
>   Hold on just second, Raoul.

As cautiously as a ninja, CHRISTINA walks to the box entrance making sure that they aren't being followed. She rubs her head in relief.

>   CHRISTINA
>   He must've gone up higher. He's
>   coming down.

She tries to close the door noticing RED DEATH coming down the stairs which RAOUL also notices. Raoul blocks the door.

>   RAOUL
>   It's him. He won't get away

>   CHRISTINA
>   In the name of our love, Raoul,
>   you'll stay right here with me.

Just because SHE asked, RAOUL obliges her.
CHRISTINA successfully closes the door.

RAOUL
Why you little liar. You've never
loved me. I must have been an idiot
to have thought that. I'm an honest
guy, Christina. I thought that you
were an honest girl, but I could
see that you were only playing some
filthy game with me.

CHRISTINA
You're gonna apologize for those
words one day, Raoul. When you do,
I'm gonna forgive you.

RAOUL
No, that's quite alright. You already
jacked up my life enough. To think
that I ever wanted to marry some
whore.

CHRISTINA
Raoul, how could you ever even think
something like that?

RAOUL [sarcastic]
Maybe I'll just hang myself.

CHRISTINA backhands him, like he was some guy
beating his wife.

CHRISTINA
I was going to tell you, but you
won't believe me. It's over.

RAOUL sees that he made a big mistake.

>   RAOUL
>   Can't you just please explain the
>   whole situation to me? You've been
>   missing for two weeks. I don't get
>   this. Even Valerie's even giving me
>   the run around.

They take off their masks.

>   CHRISTINA
>   Oh god, Babe. It's horrible.

RAOUL sees CHRISTINA with this horrifying melancholy on her face. Guilt is then seen on Raoul's face.

>   RAOUL
>   I am so sorry, Christina. I'm so
>   sorry, Please forgive me. It's just
>   that you might get killed.

>   CHRISTINA
>   Maybe, but not today.

With that said, CHRISTINA puts her mask back on.

>   CHRISTINA
>   Just please don't follow me. It's
>   dangerous.

>   RAOUL
>   But . . .

CHRISTINA
Please.

He grudgingly listens.

CUT TO . . .

INT: CHRISTINA'S DRESSING ROOM NIGHT

You see that RAOUL is behind the closet in the
dark room spying on CHRISTINA who is prepping
up for something. She has this sorrowful look
in her eyes.

CHRISTINA
Poor Erik. I hope I'm not too late.

Although he's as quiet as a mouse, the audience
sees the burning rage that growing in the eyes
of RAOUL.

From the other side of this mirror, a man's
soft voice is singing a promise song that
fits Romeo and Juliet. CHRISTINA almost seems
hypnotized by the sound of the voice.

CHRISTINA
I'm right here, Erik. I'm surprised.
You're a little late
For you.

VOICE
Fate has brought us together
I will be yours forever, Christina.

CHRISTINA goes up to the mirror. She taps it and in the mirror and she disappears.

        RAOUL
        What the hell? Who's Erik?

CHAPTER XI
STRAINED ROMANCE

FADE TO . . .

INT: VALERIE'S LIVING ROOM—NOON

VALERIE is engaging in small-talk with CHRISTINA, who doesn't look so depressed, about some movie they just saw on TV. Valerie is sick on the sofa. The doorbell rings, CHRISTINA goes to answer it. It turns out to be a surprised RAOUL. CHRISTINA smiles at him.

> CHRISTINA
> Raoul, you seem so surprised. Come on in. Make yourself at home.

RAOUL does as he is told, and VALERIE spots him giving him a motherly smile.

> VALERIE
> Raoul, I believe you know my precious adopted daughter Christina Avian.

Both CHRISTINA and RAOUL blush at that sweet comment that VALERIE said.

> VALERIE
> Hers angel brought her back to us, Raoul.

> CHRISTINA
> I thought we weren't going to talk about that. There is no such thing as the angel of music. It's just some tall tale that pa used to tell us.

VALERIE
But you took singing lessons from him for three months. You can't deny that, Chrissie.

CHRISTINA
I've already told you that someday very soon I'll explain something about this particular situation, but until then, please don't ask me any more questions about this.

VALERIE
Yeah, but only if you don't leave us, again.

CHRISTINA
This can't interest Raoul.

RAOUL gives CHRISTINA a little smile as he gently gets hold of her hands.

RAOUL
That's not quite the truth, Christina. After what had happened yesterday, I wasn't expecting to see you here. So tell me, why try to hide? Whatever it is you're hiding, I know it's not good.

VALERIE looks surprised.

VALERIE
Oh my god. Is Christina in danger?

RAOUL nods and with that, VALERIE turns toward CHRISTINA in a pleading manner.

>VALERIE
>you have to tell me everything.

She turns to RAOUL.

>VALERIE
>You have to tell what type of danger she's in.

>RAOUL
>There's something deadly all around Christina, and it's not some monster hiding in her bed.

CHRISTINA grabs a hold her step-mother's hands.

>CHRISTINA
>I'm fine, Valerie. Really, I am.

>VALERIE
>Then don't leave me again, Child.

CHRISTINA looks apologetically at VALERIE.

>CHRISTINA
>I really can't make any promise like that, Valerie. I'm sorry.

>RAOUL
>We wanna help you, but you have to let us.

CHRISTINA gets a little upset with that last comment, but she doesn't get angry.

> CHRISTINA
> I can do things by myself, Raoul. You are not my husband, and I would appreciate it if you stopped treating me like your wife. Besides, I don't even want to get married.

> RAOUL
> Well, then why are you wearing a wedding ring, Christina?

RAOUL tries to take CHRISTINA'S hand but she pulls away.

> CHRISTINA
> It's just a present.

> RAOUL
> That means you're engaged?

> CHRISTINA [angered]
> Haven't you hounded me enough?

> RAOUL
> I'm sorry. It's just that I've seen more than you think. I have.

> CHRISTINA
> Alright, out with it.

RAOUL
I saw how happy you were from the shadows of your dressing room. Erik's voice is dangerous.

RAOUL puts his face down with guilt while CHRISTINA looks at him with shock.

RAOUL
Oh my god. What did I just say?

CHRISTINA
Forget about the voice of Erik. You have to stop playing detective.

RAOUL
Is it really all that bad?

CHRISTINA
Yes, it is. Oh, Raoul promise me that you'll forget about the angel of music, and that you won't come into my room unless I invite you in.

RAOUL
Then, you have to promise me that you'll call for me soon.

CHRISTINA
I'll call you up tomorrow so we can go out for a lunch, Raoul.

RAOUL
You have my word as a southern gentleman.

CUT TO . . .

INT: CHRISTINA'S DRESSING ROOM—AFTERNOON

CHRISTINA is prepping up for her date with RAOUL, as you hear his knock on the door.

> CHRISTINA
> Just a minute.

She puts a comb through her hair, and wipes up all her makeup smudges. She then, walks to the door, opens it and finds her schoolyard sweetheart. Both of them look happy.

CUT TO . . .

INT: ITALIAN BISTRO—NOON

It's a simple joint, not too fancy. It's more like a café, than those red checkered, spaghetti places you always see in Mafia movies.

CHRISTINA and RAOUL are eating some pasta like in *Lady and the Tramp*. They are really enjoying each other.

> CHRISTINA
> . . . and Poligny said if I ever try and write a comedy again, I won't be doing anything more exciting than making him his coffee.

RAOUL gives a small chuckle.

> RAOUL
> Well are you gonna try it?

> CHRISTINA
> I doubt it.

RAOUL just stares into CHRISTINA'S eyes. CHRISTINA blushes.

> CHRISTINA
> What is it?

> RAOUL
> I'm so glad we don't have to worry about the angel of music.

> CHRISTINA
> Me to, Raoul.

CHRISTINA pecks RAOUL on the check which makes him blush happily. He pays CHRISTINA back with a kiss on her check of his own.

CUT TO . . .

INT: CHRISTINA'S DRESSING ROOM—EVENING

Small amounts of tears fall on CHRISTINA'S face. She's staring at the phone. She's not sure whether she should pick up the phone and call whoever it is she was going to call or not.

The cons of either choice seem stronger than the pros. So much so, that CRISTINA looks ill. She finally decides to pick up the phone. She dials a number and puts the phone to her ear. The phone rings for a second and then we hear RAOUL on the other line.

> RAOUL [v/o]
> Hello?

> CHRISTINA [panicky]
> Raoul, I have to talk to you. Meet me at under the Mardi Gras on the roof right away.

> RAOUL [v/o]
> Okay.

RAOUL is heard hanging up the phone as we see CHRISTINA do so. She sits back in her chair very troubled.

EXT: ROOFTOP—NIGHT

On a beautiful rooftop, A beautiful black and white Mardi Gras mask with red lips watches over all these life-size porcelain Voodoo dolls.

There's a light rain that falls on the roof as CHRISTINA is standing in between all the Voodoo dolls. RAOUL walks over to CHRISTINA from out of the shadows and into her loving arms.

Poor CHRISTINA stops holding back her tears and cries on RAOUL'S shoulder.

    RAOUL
    Christina?

CHRISTINA looks to the ground in shame.

    CHRISTINA
    Raoul, I did see you that one night
    when nobody knew I was with Erik.

    RAOUL
    Did you see me when you were riding
    in that hearse?

CHRISTINA nods.

    CHRISTINA
    Yeah . . . I did.

RAOUL'S starting to look worried again.

    RAOUL
    Christina, you have to tell me
    what's wrong, because from what
    I understand, this sounds pretty
    serious. Tell me about the first
    time you saw Erik.

    CHRISTINA
    It was the night the chandelier
    fell . . .

CHAPTER XII

KIDNAPPED BY A CORPSE

INT: CHRISTINA'S DRESSING ROOM—NIGHT

CHRISTINA walks through the door a little panicked. She shuts the door. Some soft synth-pop music is coming from her mirror.

> PHANTOM [o/s]
> Yes, it's me, Christina. It's now time for us to have our lessons face to face. Walk up to the mirror and push the glass.

The man's voice is the same one RAOUL heard. Anyway, CHRISTINA does as she is told. The mirror is actually a secret passage. She walks through it and closes the "door".

INT: SECRET HALLWAY

The hallway is filled with marble heads carved into the walls portraying grim scenes.

From behind, a gloved hand touches her shoulders. She jumps and turns around to see the long-awaited PHANTOM of the Palace with a blank, expressionless face, almost a Michael Myers like mask. She tries to scream but the Phantom cups her mouth gently.

> PHANTOM
> Oh Christina, please don't scream.
> I don't like to see you scared.

He lets go of her mouth slowly but it's obvious that she's still creeped out. The PHANTOM'S voice is very timid and shy. He takes CHRISTINA'S hand and leads her down the hallway. His timidity causes him to blabber on . . .

> PHANTOM
> Oh, please don't worry, Christina. I told them to let you sing but they wouldn't listen. I had to humiliate Carlotta. She sang like shit. And I didn't have anything to do with the chandelier.

They walk for a little while until they come across an underground lake with a boat at the edge, and they step inside the boat.

The PHANTOM stands as he paddles with a pole that has a skull-shaped head. He paddles with her watching in fear for a couple of minutes until they reach an underground house that looks an awful lot like a mausoleum. The PHANTOM parks the boat, and the two walk up to a mausoleum that the PAHNTOM calls a house.

The PHANTOM has no need for a key, so they walk right into the living room filled with music memorabilia from any era, any genre [He knows his stuff]. The PHANTOM softly shuts the door.

CUT TO . . .

INT: PHANTOM'S LIVING ROOM—NIGHT

It's some twisted paradise for any music lover. Posters and instruments abound the place. The

PHANTOM folds his arms and looks admiringly at the scared CHRISTINA.

> PHANTOM
> Don't worry, Christina. You really aren't in any kind of danger. I promise you.

CHRISTINA just stares at him like she's paralyzed with fear. Then with great fury, she tries to rip off the Phantom's mask, but he backs away in fear of rejection.

> PHANTOM
> Please don't touch the mask, Christina. I would hate to frighten you more than you already are. It's too horrid for you to set your eyes on.

CHRISTINA'S fear turns into a state of being uncomfortable. After a few moments, The PHANTOM gently takes CHRISTINA by the hand.

INT: CHRISTINA'S ROOM [Phantom's Lair]—NIGHT

It's a nice room with a rockabilly pin up theme. The strange uncomfortable feeling is still there as CHRISTINA and the PHANTOM walk in. CHRISTINA finally realizes that she's dealing with an obsessive stalker. The bastard took advantage of what her father told her.

> PHANTOM
> You had a long day, so you must be pretty tired. I've taken the

liberty to set this room up for you.
I remember one time that you said
you loved Americana so that's how I
decided to decorate it.

CHRISTINA forces herself to make a smile of
pleasure.

>CHRISTINA
>Wow. It's really cool. Thank you,
>Ang . . .

>PHANTOM
>Please call me Erik and you are so
>welcome Christina.

With that, ERIK leaves the room, and CHRISTINA
just stares at it scared to death.

CUT TO . . .

INT: ERIK'S ROOM—NIGHT

ERIK walks in and closes the door, but you see
the back of his head as he removes his blank
expressionless mask, and puts on a completely
black mask. He walks to a light switch to
tone dim the lights. He walks to this macabre
coffin filled with gothic horror imagery
presumably designed by ERIK. He lies down and
falls asleep.

CUT TO . . .

INT: ERIK'S LIVING ROOM—NIGHT

ERIK is sitting on a black, crushed velvet couch drinking a cup of coffee. It's really quite a lovely room, though with some playfully macabre eccentricities. CHRISTINA walks in.

>   ERIK [perky]
>   Well, hello, Christina. How was your
>   first night in my humble abode?

She just gazes at ERIK and starts to weep. Strangely Erik goes to comfort her.

>   ERIK
>   Oh, please don't cry. It's true
>   that I'm no angel or ghost but I am
>   miserable.

>   CHRISTINA
>   Miserable? What the hell do you know
>   of misery?

>   ERIK
>   Oh, I am miserable. I took you away
>   because I love you and I want you to
>   stay here with me. And maybe I can
>   take you out.

>   CHRISTINA
>   Then take off your mask.

She moves closer in an attempt to take it off.

>   ERIK
>   No. You shouldn't ever have to see
>   such a ghastly face, Christina.

ERIK takes CHRISTINA'S hand and leads her off.

> ERIK
> Let's go to the music room.

INT: ERIK'S MUSIC ROOM—MORNING

ERIK walks CHRISTINA into a room that looks like a music store. As scared as she is, her eyes glow when she steps in. There are bass, acoustic and electric guitars, and other instruments, like synthesizers and drum kits. CHRISTINA notices a synthesizer with some sheet music on it. She walks to it and picks up the music. It reads *Johnny Triumph*.

> CHRISTINA
> What's Johnny Triumph, Erik?

CHRISTINA'S hoping to bring him joy but it backfires.

> ERIK
> It's not good for you. How about we play a more uplifting song?

ERIK goes over to this synthesizer and starts playing.

> ERIK [singing]
> *Back in the old forest from days long gone. I would bring my flute and play this song. Never did I assume I'd ever have to leave*

*The most beautiful place where I'd
be smiling. I'd get my line and pole
and I'd go fishing*

CHRISTINA knows the song so she cautiously
joins ERIK in hopes of keeping him calm.

ERIK & CHRISTINE [singing]
*Back in the forest where you'd always
find me, we'd climb up and kiss in
the trees. Deep in the forest is
where I'd be, we'd write the most
splendid poetry*

They repeat this, and as they do, CHRISTINA
reaches slowly for ERIK'S mask, and by "the
most splendid . . ." she rips it off to reveal
a hideous skull-like face! Like some rotting
corpse hell bent on drunken vengeance, he
throws himself up.

ERIK
Oh my god! What did you do? What the
hell did you do?

ERIK grabs CHRISTINA by her top and holds her
against the wall with great rage, the rage of
a fallen angel being banished from Heaven!

ERIK
Well, you finally got to see what's
behind the mask! Do you like what
you see? Don't I look like a movie
star, like James Dean or Leonardo
DiCaprio, huh? You wanna bang me
don't you, ya vile little bitch?

Still in his terrifying rage, ERIK throws CHRISTINA down like a rag doll down to the floor. CHRISTINA'S paralyzed with great fear!

> ERIK
> So, Christina. You had to see what's behind my damn mask, didn't you? You've brought this on yourself! It's not my fault that you had to curse yourself to see the face of the dead!

ERIK drags CHRISTINA to a wall near the living room door slapping her around.

> ERIK
> Bitch! Well, Christina! You've got what you asked for. Take a look!

ERIK shoves his horrifying face in CHRISTINA'S forcing her to stare at his ghastly face! Yelling like some drunken monster, he frightens her.

> ERIK
> Feast your eyes on ugliness unsurpassed, but take a long damn look so the horrific image will forever last! Look at me! Look at ME! You wanted to see my face, so damn it, here's your chance!

Still in his fit of rage, ERIK throws CHRISTINA in the living room and slams the door in her face. ERIK walks up to this clothed object.

He rips off the cloth to reveal a mirror and crashes it with his Fists of Fury.

FADE TO . . .

INT: APARTMENT LIVING ROOM—NIGHT

It's long time ago during the sixties or seventies. A young ERIK is watching *House on Haunted Hill* with Vincent Price, while a lady is wrapping a box up.

SUPER: November 1st 1987 "Day of the Dead"

>   LADY
>   Erik?
>
>   ERIK
>   Yeah, Mom?
>
>   MOTHER
>   I've got you a birthday gift.

ERIK walks over to his mom, who gives the package as she lights up a cigarette nonchalantly.

ERIK looks really excited, joy fills his face. He rips the package open. His expression transforms from joy to bitterness, as he finds a homemade leather mask.

>   MOTHER
>   That's better. Now, I don't have
>   look at a goddamned corpse all the
>   time.

ERIK [sarcastic]
Gee, thanks, Mom. Now I have a reason
to kill you.

ERIK'S mom just laughs. She knows that he
isn't going to do anything.

MOTHER
Where are you going to go after?

Erik looks around for a quick answer. He sees an
advertisement in a magazine; an advertisement
for some sideshow. For the odd, freakish
looking people, come join!

He also sees a knife right by the article.

ERIK
I'll join the circus.

ERIK grabs the knife and throws it at his own
mother.

ERIK
There, now you can burn in Hell
instead of have a dead thing for a
son.

MOTHER
No!

ERIK rushes out of the house and comes right
back in with an axe. He walks up to his dying
mother, and hacks off her head. After he does
this, the kid bursts into uncontrollable
sobs.

INT: ERIK'S MUSIC ROOM—NIGHT

The faded colors return, but not the full colors. Erik rushes past the mirror, and walks to a case of CDs and boom box with a lot of stickers of rock bands of the darker, brooding variety. He rips out a burnt CD with the words *Johnny Triumph*.

This is obviously what ERIK tried to refrain from showing CHRISTINA. If Hell ever were to have a soundtrack, then this would be it, with horribly distorted guitars playing the most melancholy riffs. ERIK puts it on full blast knowing full well that CHRISTINA has no other choice than to listen to Hell itself.

INT: LIVING ROOM

Being stuck in the living room, CHRISTINA knows that she has no other choice than to listen to the sick tragedy of riffs that belong to *Johnny Triumph*. At first, she's repulsed by the morbid riffs, but after a while, she starts to have empathy for ERIK. She walks in the door to the music room.

INT: MUSIC ROOM

CHRISTINA closes the door and walks over to ERIK. She taps him on the shoulder while he has his head laid down in his arms. He puts the boom box on pause.

      ERIK
      What do you want, bitch?

CHRISTINA
Erik, if I start to tremble it's not because I'm scared or disgusted by you.

ERIK
Then why do you do it, my dear beloved?

CHRISTINA
It's because we're so much alike. I also feel like society's betrayed me. Your face doesn't scare me anymore.

ERIK listens with curiosity.

CHRISTINA [cont'd]
And I think that when you love someone, you get angered with them when you don't want to see them get hurt. To me, you have a wonderful heart.

ERIK kneels at CHRISTINA'S feet, but she has her eyes closed. She can't stand the sight of him. She's lying through her teeth.

ERIK
Christina, I'm so sorry. I never meant to blow up like that, but I did, because I knew that if you saw my face, that I would just scare you even more.

CHRISTINA
It's okay, Erik.

ERIK
If there's anything that I can do
for you, please ask me.

EXT: ROOFTOP—NIGHT

CHRISTINA
. . . and I finally got him to take
me out at night. The night you saw
me in the hearse was the night that
he let me go.

RAOUL
Why would he just let you when he
held you prisoner?

CHRISTINA
Well, I promised Erik that I'd visit
him.

RAOUL
Well, are you really going to visit
that psychopath again, Chrissie?

CHRISTINA
I already have, remember? It was
the night of the Mardi Gras party?
When you spied on me heard me talk
to him.

RAOUL
Okay.

CHRISTINA
Raoul, you got to get me out of here.
I tried killing myself to try and

get away from Erik but he stopped me. Get me out if here.

RAOUL
Tomorrow night, this Erik will be nothing more than a bad dream, Christina. I promise.

CHRISTINA
I have to see Erik one more time, though. How about the following morning?

RAOUL
Oh come on, Christina. You have to work with me here, babe. Let's just get this over with.

CHRISTINA
Alright, alright. Tomorrow night, get me out of New Orleans.

RAOUL
Anywhere in the entire world.

CHRISTINA
Brazil?

RAOUL
We'll go to Brazil.

RAOUL and CHRISTINA give each other a mildly passionate kiss, and CHRISTINA gets out of there. RAOUL follows her really closely as she tells him to. They race literally for their lives.

INT: PALACE STAIRCASE

It's a windy staircase with the bars to hold it up shaped like bones.

CHRISTINA and RAOUL make it down to the stairs but when they reach it, CHRISTINA looks at her hand. She looks totally worried.

>   CHRISTINA
>   Oh God. No.

>   RAOUL
>   What is it? What's wrong?

>   CHRISTINA
>   It's Erik's ring. I think I dropped
>   it on the rooftop.

>   RAOUL
>   Why is that so bad?

>   CHRISTINA
>   He doesn't know that I'm in love with
>   you. He told me that the day the ring
>   is off, and then he'll disown me.

RAOUL just looks at CHRISTINA with an upset firmness.

>   RAOUL
>   Do you really have to have the ring?

>   CHRISTINA
>   But If I don't have the ring, he'll
>   kill us both.

RAOUL
Well, what is he going to do?

PERSIAN [o/s]
It doesn't matter. Forget the ring.

RAOUL and CHRISTINA turn around to find the tall menacing figure of the PERSIAN coming down the stairs.

RAOUL
What do you mean?

PERSIAN
It's just not safe, ma'am. That's all.

CHRISTINA
But you don't understand. I really need to go look for my . . .

PERSIAN
Your ring that the Phantom gave you?

CHRISTINA looks at him curiously.

CHRISTINA
Yeah, how the hell did you know that?

The PERSIAN just stands there firmly almost suspiciously. Then he reaches into his leather jacket pocket, pulls out CHRISTINA'S ring and then he hands it to her.

PERSIAN
I just know, and let's leave this
conversation at that.

The PERSIAN walks off and the couple just
looks at each other.

CHRISTINA
Whoa. Back up there a second, there.
That was just plain weird, Raoul.

RAOUL
You won't get any argument from me.

Chapter XIII

Back with the Kidnapper

INT: SECRET PASSAGE

It's dark, rocky place filled with carvings of skulls and other dastardly images. The PERSIAN is walking around cautiously. He's looking for ERIK.

He lights himself up a cigarette. He goes a little deeper into the passage, leading to an underground lake.

INT: UNDERGROUND LAKE

The PERSIAN enters. It's a creepy looking swamp like area, filled with vines and fireflies lighting it like a tattered blanket of stars.

The PERSIAN looks around, and some beautiful yet haunting music being performed by some young women is being played at the other side of the lake where ERIK'S horrid mausoleum like house is. The music is seems almost hypnotic. A pale gas comes out of a canister causing the drug induced trance. He tries to swim over to the music. It takes the PERSIAN a while to get near. He swims closer to the Siren melody.

When suddenly, gloved hand a pops out of the water out of the water, reaches for the PERSIAN'S neck, and starts to strangle the poor guy. The rest of the hand's body pops up to reveal ERIK.

Once ERIK realizes he's choking the PERSIAN, he stops and takes him over to his underground house.

INT: ERIK'S KITCHEN—NIGHT

The PERSIAN is warming up by a heater, while ERIK is pouring some tea for the PERSIAN. ERIK seems warm and comfortable. They clearly have a history with each other. ERIK lights up a cigarette and leans closer to the PERSIAN and grabs his shoulders like an old buddy.

> ERIK
> Had I not recognized you, you would have been sleeping with the fishes, amigo. So, why have you showed up all the way in New Orleans after so long? It's been, what, ten years?

> PERSIAN
> There's been enough brutality to catch the eye of Interpol. Since I know you, I volunteered myself for the case.

> ERIK
> There has to be a little more than that.

> PERSIAN
> Just come down to my office. I could get you some help, Erik. Maybe even surgery.

> ERIK
> No. I'm content where I am right here.

> PERSIAN
> Then were you the one behind the
> fall of the chandelier?

ERIK starts to chuckle warmly.

> ERIK
> The rope they used to hook it up,
> just wasn't made that well.

> PERSIAN
> I just have one more question,
> then.

> ERIK
> Shoot.

> PERSIAN
> Why are you doing this? One day, you
> won't be able to stop yourself.

> ERIK
> Murders will lead to more murders?

> PERSIAN
> Yeah, that's what I'm saying. You
> know that there has been too much
> as it is.

ERIK gives out another chuckle, a much more
sinister one as he stares into the PERSIAN'S
eyes. ERIK takes a big drag of his cigarette.

> ERIK
> Then, tell that to my mother who
> took my life with her dread of her

forsaken, cadaver of a son. Murder isn't always merely forcing someone else's heartbeat to stop beating for good. You should know that.

PERSIAN
Erik. I know. I'm not saying she . . .

ERIK
You're not saying that's right? You have never been in that situation. So, how the hell would you know how it feels to be rejected by your own mother?

PERSIAN
Oh, Come on, Erik.

ERIK
Don't tell me what to do, okay?

INT: CHRISTINA'S DRESSING ROOM—EVENING

CHRISTINA and RAOUL are there along with SPECIAL AGENT MIFROID. They are all drinking some sort of beverage. MIFROID finishes up a cigar. MIFROID is pleading with CHRISTINA to get some bodyguards.

MIFROID
Are you absolutely certain that you'd rather me not put out a couple of best guys onstage with you? They'll be behind the curtains.

CHRISTINA
Yes. I am one hundred percent positive. No guards on stage with me.

RAOUL
But what if Erik does show up, Christina? Just a couple of them, Babe.

CHRISTINA
He'll only be in his box. Trust me. He is never ever in anywhere else.

MIFROID
Okay, then. I'll just have the boxkeeper make a citizen's arrest.

That should clear everything up real fast.

CHRISTINA
She'll never make the arrest. Erik always makes serving him a pleasure, and she's loyal to good customers.

RAOUL
What do you think we should do?

CHRISTINA
Just leave Erik alone. That's all. If we leave him alone, then he'll leave us alone. It's as simple as that.

MIFROID shakes his head, and lights up a cigar.

MIFROID
Oh, forget it. I doubt this Erik
character even exists.

CHRISTINA
Fine. If you don't want to be here,
that's fine with me. The door is
right there. Just make sure you
don't let it hit you in the ass on
your way out.

RAOUL
Christina?!

CHRISTINA
Do you trust me, Raoul?

RAOUL
Yes . . .

CHRISTINA
Then, let's keep it that way. I really
do know what I'm doing, alright?

MIFROID [under his breath]
Good. That leaves me two less
schizoids to deal with.

RAOUL gives MIFROID a little Birdie as he
walks ou.

RAOUL
What that was about?

    CHRISTINA
I know Erik well enough to know that
if we try to apprehend him, it's more
likely that he'll put the palace in
danger, so the safer route would-be
to leave Erik.

    RAOUL
Are you sure about this? I mean I
don't want to take any chances.

    CHRISTINA
I am one hundred percent positive
that this is what I want to do. Now
if you'll excuse me, I have to talk
to Richards and Moncharmin.

CHRISTINA gets up, gives RAOUL a small kiss on
the cheek, walks out the door, and heads for
the managers' office.

    RAOUL [to himself]
What am I going to do with you?

INT: MANAGERS' OFFICE—EVENING

The menacing PERSIAN and the two managers are
having a little disagreement about security.
The managers want tons and the PERSIAN thinks
it should be on the down low. CHRISTINA walks
in like a fire ready to go wild. She spots the
PERSIAN, and she walks over to him.

    CHRISTINA
Excuse me, Sir, but I really need to
have a quick chat with my managers

right now, so if you could just please excuse yourself? Sorry.

The PERSIAN takes a look at CHRISTINA, and then he turns to the two managers, then back at CHRISTINA. He gives her a little nod.

PERSIAN
I think that I could pull that off, Miss Avian. I'll be back

EXIT PERSIAN and the managers turn to CHRISTINA.

RICHARDS
Now, what can we do for you?

CHRISTINA
Has box five been sold yet?

RICHARDS
Nope.

CHRISTINA
Good. I really need to leave box five empty for tonight.

MONCHARMIN
And just why do you need that? Do you believe in the Phantom of the Palace?

CHRISTINA starts to hesitate for a second or two, but she thinks up something to say pretty quickly, however.

> CHRISTINE
> Not really. It's just that I have a
> friend who said that he would like
> to have it. That's pretty much it
> the deal here.

MONCHARMIN and RICHARDS smile at her, chuckling
pleasantly with good will.

> MONCHARMIN
> Well, in that case, box five will be
> completely at your friend's disposal
> for tonight, Christina. Hope your
> guest enjoys the show tonight.

> RICHARDS
> And thank you for letting us in on the
> little secret about your friend.

> CHRISTINA
> You are very welcome, and thank
> you for giving my friend the box
> tonight. I'll be seeing you around,
> gentlemen. Perhaps later tonight.

She shakes her managers' hands and walks out
the door. We all spot a portrait. The eyes
disappear and other eyes that actually seem to
fit the portrait better appear to reveal that
somebody was spying on the conversation. Could
it be ERIK?

CUT TO . . .

INT: CHRISTINA'S DRESSING ROOM—EVENING

CHRISTINA is getting reading for her performance of JOHNNY FAUST. She has the role Anna Carlotta portrayed; during the tragic incident with the chandelier, the sinister succubus who does the devil's dirty work by buying JOHNNY FAUST'S soul.

What makes her interpretation of the succubus different from CARLOTTA is that she only suggests her sensuality, not at all appearing as slutty, going for the more subtle, almost vampiric form of a demon. So of course her costume reflects this.

CUT TO . . .

EXT: BOX FIVE—EVENING

MRS. GIRY is obviously attending the box, standing there when a mysterious looking man walks up to her. This man's eyes have no white and the skin is extremely pale. Almost like a latex mask with a vague plain ordinary face. Of course, it's ERIK.

>ERIK
>Excuse me, ma'am, is this box five?

MRS. GIRY turns to see this mysterious looking guy, who seems pretty creepy.

>MRS. GIRY
>Well, that depends, man. Who's asking for the information Mon Ami?

ERIK gives her a little chuckle as he shakes the hand of MRS. GIRY.

> ERIK
> Oh just friend of the voodoo palace ghost is asking. My name is Erik.

> MRS. GIRY
> So, you know the Phantom, Erik? What's your relation with him, Kid?

> ERIK
> I'm only his valet. I run all of his errands for him and stuff. I only show up if he isn't up to going. He wants you to keep him in high regards so he sends me to give you your tips and everything.

> MRS. GIRY
> That sounds a little far fetched, Mon Ami.

> ERIK
> Yeah, but then again doesn't some dead guy who haunts the Palace sound pretty far-fetched too?

There's something about him that MRS. GIRY recognizes. The voice is pretty menacing but pleasant ironically. The clothes are grim but also very fashionable. So, the Phantom has a new mask, does he?

MRS. GIRY
So, that's the face behind the mask,
huh, Erik?

ERIK
Excuse me?

MRS. GIRY
So, when did you get a new latex
masque?

ERIK
I'm sorry, but I don't quite follow
you.

MRS. GIRY just shrugs.

MRS. GIRY
Do you know the Persian?

Okay, now it's time for Erik to play along.

ERIK
Oh yeah. For 15 years. He works for
Interpole.

MRS. GIRY
He said he knew you. But never did
he mention that you wore latex mask,
monsieur. It's a very fitting one.

ERIK looks at her threateningly. He doesn't
look too happy.

ERIK
How the hell did you know who I
was?

MRS. GIRY
Honey, you've been coming to this
here box for so long, that it could
not have been anybody else.

ERIK
If you ever tell anyone a single
thing . . .

MRS. GIRY just looks at ERIK like he needs to
take himself on a trip to a mental institution
or something. Then she smiles at ERIK.

MRS. GIRY
Tell? Are you crazy? Why the hell
would I rat on someone who treats
his box keeper so well? You can
commit the darkest of crimes but
if you scratch my back, I scratch
yours. Oui?

ERIK
Thanks for not telling anyone,
Mrs. Giry. I really appreciate it.
Mercy.

MRS. GIRY
You are very welcome, now get yourself
a seat in there and enjoy your show.
Oh, by the way, that Christina Avian
is a real looker too.

ERIK smiles up at MRS. GIRY as he takes his seat in his box.

> ERIK
> I know. Thank you.

CUT TO . . .

INT: PALACE MAIN STAGE—NIGHT

The stage is once again set up in a hellish manner. JOHNNY FAUST also looks frightened again. CHRISTINA comes out of the same trap-door with same black metal riff that CARLOTTA entered the scene to, and she starts singing her part.

> CHRISTINA [singing]
> *Johnny. What can I get you honey? I can grant you about anything Your little heart desires.*

Suddenly, at that last line, the room's lights go out as does the band's instruments. When the lights come back on, CHRISTINA is nowhere to be found.

Chapter XIV

The Hunt For Christina

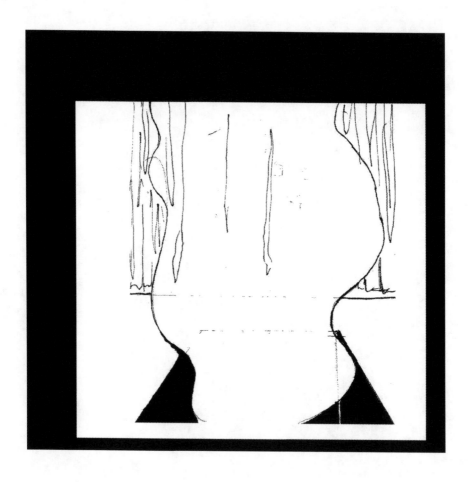

INT: SECRET PASSAGE

An uncomfortable CHRISTINA is accompanying the disguised ERIK. ERIK rips off his latex mask to reveal his more corpse-like face. ERIK picks up a white theater mask to put on. He runs off with the girl he loves, and she silent out of fear.

> ERIK
> Come on, Christina. I would like nothing more than to hear you sing.

INT: PRIVATE BOX—NIGHT

This box just so happens to belong to RICHARDS and MONCHARMIN.

> MONCHARMIN
> Well, our Phantom's back in action.

> RICHARDS
> Oh my mother lovin' god . . . Answer me one thing.

MONCHARMIN contemplates this just for a second, and then he looks curiously at RICHARDS.

> MONCHARMIN
> Shoot.

> RICHARDS
> Why in the black hell did the Phantom have to strike tonight?

MONCHARMIN drops his head in a confused frustration, and shrugs his shoulders.

> MONCHARMIN
> I don't really have any idea whatsoever how to answer that.

> RICHARDS
> I thought not.

CUT TO . . .

EXT: PRIVATE BOX—NIGHT

RAOUL walks out of his box with a great rage, walking right past the PERSIAN, who grabs Raoul's shoulder before he goes too far.

> PERSIAN
> Hold on a second, there, Mr. De Chagny.

RAOUL turns around grudgingly. He is definitely in no mood for chit-chat, but he thinks that the PERSIAN might know a thing or tow about what had happened. Still, Raoul's not sure if he could actually trust the PERSIAN or not making the decision difficult.

> RAOUL
> You're the Persian, aren't you?

> PERSIAN
> Yup. That's me alright.

RAOUL
Well, unless you happen to be interested in helping me out or you could pull Christina Avian out your magic hat, I really see no reason for to stay and chat.

PERSIAN
Would helping get her back from Erik count as both, Mr. de Chagny.

Okay. That did it. The PERSIAN now has RAOUL'S attention.

RAOUL
What do you know about Erik?

PERSIAN
Erik and I go way back. Since I have known him long enough, I could provide you with his secrets. You need me to.

The PERSIAN hands RAOUL a gun; pulls one out for himself, and they cock it back. RAOUL lowers his, and in frustrated, the PERSIAN grabs RAOUL'S arm in front of his face.

PERSIAN
Always keep it at eye level.

Hurriedly, RAOUL agrees.

RAOUL
Alright. Let's go get my girl back. Where to we start?

The PERSIAN smiles devilishly at RAOUL.

> PERSIAN
> Christina's dressing room.

> RAOUL
> Okay. Let's go then.

EXT: CHRISTINA'S DRESSING ROOM

The PERSIAN and RAOUL make it, but the closer they get to the door, the more closely to the shadows they walk. The more cautiously they walk. They're in total stealth mode. The PERSIAN opens the door, slowly as to be prepared for anything.

INT: DRESSING ROOM

Our two heroes walk in, and the PERSIAN closes the door behind themselves, gently, softly.

> RAOUL
> We've made it this far, what now?

The PERSIAN isn't quite sure what to do, as he turns on a small flashlight and looks around the room. The PERSIAN walks up to the mirror that he saw his beloved CHRISTINA disappear into.

> PERSIAN
> Erik loves using secret passages.
> This mirror here should be one.

RAOUL
I should have known.

PERSIAN
What?

RAOUL
I saw Christina go through it, but
I couldn't figure out what the
hell that mirror thing was at all.
Christina was in a trance.

PERSIAN
Hmm. Erik must have been singing a
ballad to Christina.

The PERSIAN pushes a strange, red skull on the
mirror's frame to reveal the hidden hallway
into a dark cavernous passageway. Our two heroes
step forward with a suspecting eye through the
mirror door.

INT: SECRET HALLWAY

It's dark, with the PERSIAN'S little flashlight
above his berretta, which sheds just enough
light to safely walk through. Though rocks
strangely shaped like giant skulls fill the
walls.

Foolishly jumping before he thinks, RAOUL
tries to walk down the path that leads to
the underground lake but the PERSIAN grabs
him by the shirt and throws him away from the
lake.

PERSIAN
Where are you going?

RAOUL
I'm going to Erik's hideout to kick
that sex fiend's ass.

PERSIAN
That's the wrong way then.

RAOUL
What do you mean?

PERSIAN
That's the wrong way.

RAOUL looks at the PERSIAN with heavy
annoyance.

RAOUL
And what exactly is wrong with going
to this underground lake?

PERSIAN
Well, I tried talking to Erik after
your bout with Christina on the
rooftop. And . . . well, it just
not safe. And let's just leave it
at that.

RAOUL
Then where do we go then?

PERSIAN
The torture chamber.

RAOUL gets a little creeped out by those last three words, but he releases his fear with logic.

>RAOUL
>The torture chamber? And the lake isn't safe?

>PERSIAN
>At least with the torture chamber, we have a fighting chance to survive.

>RAOUL
>Okay, what are they?

>PERSIAN
>We have to go through it to help me remember.

RAOUL puts his head down in frustration, grabs the PERSIAN by his shirt.

>RAOUL
>You better be sure.

>PERSIAN
>What choices have we?

With a hunch that the PERSIAN'S right, he lets go and holds out his arm granting the PERSIAN the ability to lead the way.

>RAOUL
>Okay then, let's do it.

> PERSIAN
> You really would do anything for her wouldn't you?

RAOUL nods.

> PERSIAN
> Even die?

> RAOUL
> Yes.

> PERSIAN
> Good.

Of course, RAOUL gets uncomfortable by the PERSIAN saying that, as he starts to breathe heavily with fear.

They walk down some stairs and the designs on the walls are pretty gruesome with skulls and ghosts carved on the wall. Paintings of screaming cupids and children over flow the other side. It's the work of the morbid artist that we all know ERIK to be. RAOUL is appalled by the gruesome imagery while the PERSIAN stares grimly ahead as he walks forward.

> RAOUL
> What sick, psychotic bastard could ever come up with these horrible images? He must be a demon straight from hell.

PERSIAN
This is only the way to the torture
chamber. That's all. It's his idea
of décor.

RAOUL looks at the PERSIAN and he is obviously
afraid, but he can't let CHRISTINA down.

Chapter XV

The Scorpion
+
The Cricket

INT: CHRISTINA'S ROOM (Erik's Lair]

While CHRISTINA is handcuffed to her bed and ERIK paces around the frantically with a million conflicting thoughts. CHRISTINA just stares in fear and dread at the wall, paralyzed by her fear. ERIK turns and notices how scared she is. Her fear causes him to turn away in self shame and guilt.

> ERIK
> Oh, Christina. I had to lock you up like that, because we just can't have you attempt suicide again. I don't want you to kill yourself. You're much too precious to me. I only want to settle down. Is that so hard to understand?

> CHRISTINA
> No, that isn't, Erik.

> ERIK
> All I have to do is wear my latex mask and I could take you out in public, because I could look close enough to everybody else with it on. You saw that mask just now, remember my dear?

> CHRISTINA
> I remember, Erik.

> ERIK
> I wouldn't hurt you.

INT: CHAMBER STAIRWAY'S END

The hall is filled with gruesome wax displays of horrible crimes and vicious murders, all done in a camp macabre sort of way. It gives you chills and thrills and entertainment. The PERSIAN looks at all these wax statues and a tear of nostalgia falls from his eyes. RAOUL, on the other hand, just wants to move forward.

RAOUL and the PERSIAN make it to this door with a sign reading "Beware of the Rodent Man. Enter at your own risk."

They look at each other with great discomfort. The heroes move cautious though they may be.

>   PERSIAN
>   Well, are you ready, Mr. De Chagny?

>   RAOUL
>   God, I hope so.

CUT TO . . .

INT: RAT CHAMBER

They walk inside to this dark room, and they walk for a little while not expecting anything drastic, When out of nowhere, they see this flaming head. Obviously, not even the PERSIAN knows what to do. On top of that, the chamber is filled with this wretched noise, like squeals of the unknown.

            PERSIAN
            Oh, shit.

RAOUL has this weird feeling in his stomach,
with those last two words, and RAOUL looks at
the PERSIAN.

            RAOUL
            Ah, shit. Why did you just say
            that?

            PERSIAN
            I don't remember Erik talking about
            this room at all.

The flaming head comes closer, and Raoul is
about to have a nervous breakdown.

            RAOUL
            What are we gonna do?

The flaming head gets close enough to reveal
it's only some guy holding a lantern. It's
just the rat catcher.

            RAT CATCHER
            Just let me and my rats mosey on
            along. We don't mean any harm. Watch
            your step. Make sure you don't step
            on any rats.

The PERSIAN makes a sigh of relief. He finally
remembers ERIK telling him about the rat
catcher.

> PERSIAN
> Don't worry. Your rats will be fine.
> Just keep moving.

CUT TO . . .

INT: DARK HALLWAY

This is the first "normal" looking cave, though they can barely see a thing even with the PERSIAN'S flashlight. Still, RAOUL and the PERSIAN are making remarkable progress, slowly but surely. The PERSIAN see that RAOUL lowered his gun soothe PERSIAN shoves his hand up in front of his eyes.

> PERSIAN
> Keep your gun at eye level.

> RAOUL
> Why do I have to do that?

> PERSIAN
> It's really the only way to defend yourself against the Punjab lasso.

> RAOUL
> What's the Punjab lasso?

> PERSIAN
> It's a material called catgut.

They come across a brand new chamber. This chamber is filled with stylized dead rotting trees all over the place over all these tombstones around them. From each tree a

noose is tied for a quick escape from the grim
torture.

CUT TO . . .

INT: TREE CHAMBER

The PERSIAN and RAOUL walk into the room,
cautiously waiting for anything come and attack.
They move slowly about trying to figure out
what part of ERIK'S terrible lair they're in.

After looking around for a few moments, a
sense of dread comes across the PERSIAN. He
realizes that they've made it.

> PERSIAN
> I am totally stupid.

> RAOUL
> Where are we?

> PERSIAN
> We now are in the torture chamber,
> Mr. De Chagny.

> RAOUL
> So, we've finally made it? Just how
> do you know that?

INT: CHRISTINA'S ROOM [Erik's Lair]

Though ERIK is a cruel monster, it's almost
plain to see that he cares for CHRISTINA, even
if it's for his own greedy agenda. He's an
obsessive wretch.

> ERIK
> Are the locks too tight? If they
> are, I loosen them. I don't want to
> hurt you, Christina.

CHRISTINA forces a smile to give to ERIK,
trying to cover up all the agonizingly horrible
fear that's growing inside of her.

> CHRISTINA
> they're fine, Erik.

As they are talking, you hear RAOUL and the
PERSIAN through the hallow walls around the
house. CHRISTINA gets extremely frightened at
this point as ERIK becomes more sinister.

> ERIK
> Well, my darling. It looks as though
> we have some visitors. Raoul and the
> Persian perhaps?

> PERSIAN [o/s]
> Eric worked for an Iranian president
> before here. In the president's
> mansion, he's created a torture
> chamber using mirrors and heaters.

> RAOUL [o/s]
> Yeah, but how do you know we're
> finally in the torture chamber,
> though?

CHRISTINA looks worried as Erik walks to a
control panel and ERIK presses in them in some
combo.

ERIK
This is how you know you are in my
torture chamber, Mr. De Chagny. This
is how you know.

INT: TORTURE CHAMBER

The PERSIAN and RAOUL look at all of the nooses
that hanging from the trees. They seem lot
more pleasant than the horror ERIK plans for
our poor heroes.

PERSIAN
Erik probably knows we're down
here.

RAOUL
Are those Punjab lassoes?

PERSIAN
Yeah. Erik sent them down so we could
have some form of escape from this
torture.

RAOUL
This guy's real sick. He is just
sick!

The PERSIAN laughs in amusement.

PERSIAN
Yeah, but aren't we all a bit deranged
whenever we feel truly threatened?

INT: CHRISTINA'S ROOM [Erik's Lair}

CHRISTINA is scared while ERIK seems to be enjoying this sick form of torture. She watches in terror as he taunts them and mocks them.

> ERIK
> Now, if you'll just excuse for a minute, I'm going to prepare a little deadly game for the two of you.

> CHRISTINA
> Erik, if you love me then, please. Don't hurt them down there.

> ERIK
> Oh, their fate rests entirely in your hands, my dear. Not mine.

CHRISTINA can't believe all the monstrous things she is hearing. Why did Erik have to say that?

EXIT ERIK laughing at the grim situation.

> CHRISTINA
> Raoul? Can you hear me?

INT: TORTURE CHAMBER

ERIK must have really turned up the heat, because RAOUL and the PERSIAN are panting miserably; worse than dogs.

> RAOUL
> Oh god. The nooses are just right there. Can't we just end the torture now?

PERSIAN
Shut up and listen for while. I think
I hear your girlfriend.

INT: CHRISTINA'S ROOM [Erik's Lair]

RAOUL [o/s]
Christina? Is that you?

CHRISTINA
Yes, it's me. Where are you, Honey?

RAOUL [o/s]
I'm in Erik's torture chamber.

CHRISTINA Shudders in fear. She paces all
around the room trying to figure out what to
do.

CHRISTINA
I'm going to try and get Erik to set
you free. Just hold on.

A few moments pass and ERIK returns with a
small black bag for CHRISTINA which he puts on
the bed.

CHRISTINA
Erik?

ERIK turns to face CHRISTINA.

ERIK
Yeah?

    CHRISTINA
    The chains are getting too tight.
    Do you think you could take them off
    for a while?

    ERIK
    Sure.

He takes a key out of jacket pocket and unlocks
the cuffs.

    ERIK
    And now, my dear, I would like you
    to do me a favor.

ERIK takes out of his bag, two remote controls.
They each have a painting of a creature on
them. One has a scorpion while the other has
a cricket.

    ERIK
    Press the cricket, the palace will
    blow up. If you press the scorpion,
    our guests won't eve.

CHRISTINA is shocked. It's too tough of a
decision.

    CHRISTINA
    Why do you put me through this hell,
    Erik? You're doing nothing more than
    hurting innocent people?

ERIK
Yes, I do see that, and I wouldn't
do that if they would just learn to
stay out my way.

He grabs hold of her hands gently.

ERIK [cont'd]
So, please just choose the scorpion.
Just fear me, love me, do as I say
and I will be your slave.

CHRISTINA
Why do this to me? This is too
painful.

ERIK
All I want is to take you out on
Sundays. With my latex mask, I look
just look just like a normal person.
You don't even have to be sincere
about your love.

CHRISTINA is feeling totally nauseated.

CHRISTINA
I can't choose.

ERIK is getting a little irritated, though
it's tender to her.

ERIK
Your delay irritates me. Choose.

CHRISTINA
I can't, you bastard!

> ERIK [screaming]
> Make your choice now!

CHRISTINA is horrified. ERIK is too upset already. If she doesn't choose ERIK would choose for her, and choose the cricket.

> CHRISTINA [trembling]
> The scorpion, Erik. I choose you.

Out of nothing more than fear and panic, CHRISTINA chooses to press the remote with the scorpion.

INT: TORTURE CHAMBER

Just as CHRISTINA pushes the scorpion, water starts to come out of the walls. The PERSIAN and RAOUL loose any cool they had.

> RAOUL
> Oh, god! How the hell are we ever going to get out of this?

> PERSIAN
> I don't know, but if we don't, we're as good as dead.

> RAOUL
> Dammit! I was hoping you wouldn't say that!

INT: CHRISTINA'S ROOM [Erik's Lair]

CHRISTINA is still trembling. Now, not only is she trembling in fear but also with the greatest guilt a single person could ever know.

> ERIK
> Now, that wasn't so hard, was it?

> CHRISTINA
> No. Now what about them?

> ERIK
> Now, if you'll excuse me . . .

ERIK knows that CHRISTINA'S rescuers are about to drown. However, that was never ERIK'S intention. He must go into the torture chamber and rescue them. They'll probably wish that they had drowned though.

INT: TORTURE CHAMBER

ERIK gets to it through a door in his house. However, from the torture chamber, it appears to be nothing more than a tree. The PERSIAN and RAOUL are nearly drowning. ERIK has to act fast.

He goes underwater, and he finds a wheel that drains the water into a tunnel. He struggles to turn the wheel, but finally succeeds in draining out the chamber.

As it's draining out, he leads his prisoners to the tree with the door. They enter, ERIK carrying them on his shoulders.

Chapter XVI

The Eulogy

INT: PRIVATE TORTURE CELL

ERIK ties up the victims to a pole. There are a lot of whips, an iron maiden, and a torture rack in the room. So, obviously he still isn't going to play nice. ERIK ties them up to the wall. He then leaves to be with CHRISTINA.

INT: CHRISTINA'S ROOM [Erik's Lair]

ERIK takes his mask off, and kisses CHRISTINA on her forehead. He seems a little forlorn. He reaches into his jacket pocket, pulls out some keys, and he gives them to CHRISTINA.

> ERIK
> Just get out of here. Take Mr. De Chagny and the Persian with you. Beat it.

> CHRISTINA
> Why the hell are you doing this for me?

> ERIK
> Because . . . I want to.

> CHRISTINA
> Okay, but the hell why do you want to?

> ERIK
> Because, nobody has ever showed me love, let alone let me kiss them, not even my own mother. Now, get out of here, so I can rest in piece.

CHRISTINA finally sees beyond ERIK'S face, and his crimes, and sees his beautiful broken heart.

EXT: PERSIAN'S HOUSE—NIGHT

It's a nice place, though very simple and humble. With just a few roses, it doesn't stand out all that much. With his latex mask, ERIK walks slowly up to the door and rings the bell. The PERSIAN answers a few minutes later. He looks surprised, but invites ERIK in.

INT: PERSIAN'S LIVING ROOM

The interior is just as humble though there are a few pieces of Iranian artwork hanging on the wall. ERIK and the PERSIAN are inside sitting down.

>   PERSIAN
>   Is the killing spree over Erik?
>
>   ERIK
>   I still have one murder to make, and
>   it's not yours. Don't worry.
>
>   PERSIAN
>   What do you mean?
>
>   ERIK
>   Have you heard the term "Seppuku"?
>
>   PERSIAN
>   No.

ERIK
It's a ritualistic suicide in Japan.

PERSIAN
So, you're just gonna kill yourself?

ERIK
Christina has showed the most compassion that anybody ever gave me. It's my way of ending the horror. I'll be watching you in Hell, Copper.

With that, ERIK pulls out a gun and shoots himself, a bloody ghost of what used to be hate and madness. The PERSIAN just stands there as tears fall from his sympathetic eyes.

PERSIAN
I'll still be around old friend.

The End . . .

MUSIC AND MADNESS

I hear her beautiful song in my nightmare

Seeing my death face would make her scream

And I stalk the shadows like some dark angel

Humanity has been cruel and I'm so vengeful